WAITING FOR
WOVOKA

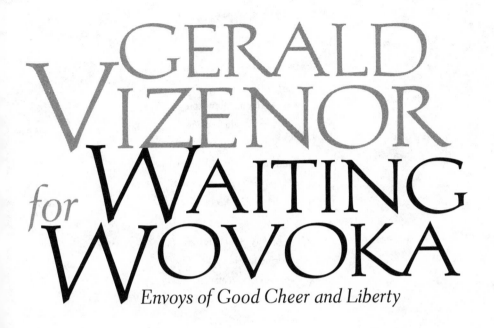

GERALD VIZENOR

for WAITING WOVOKA

Envoys of Good Cheer and Liberty

WESLEYAN UNIVERSITY PRESS

>> <<

MIDDLETOWN, CONNECTICUT

WESLEYAN UNIVERSITY PRESS
Middletown CT 06459
www.wesleyan.edu/wespress
© 2023 Gerald Vizenor
All rights reserved
Manufactured in the United States of America
Designed and typeset in Parkinson Electra
by Eric M. Brooks

Library of Congress
Cataloging-in-Publication Data
available at https://catalog.loc.gov/
cloth ISBN 978-08195-0042-7
paper ISBN 978-08195-0043-4
ebook ISBN 978-08195-0044-1

5 4 3 2 1

CONTENTS

Hand Puppet Parleys

Waiting for
Wovoka

SLIGHT HESITATIONS

Truman La Chance was a contrary heir of the ancient fur trade and a native orphan stranded in the dreary ruins of civilization. He was silent, solitary, and learned by nature how to sidetrack the crafty circle of separatists with heart stories and dream songs, and how easily he could turn aside overnight healers, federal agents, and timber barons with tricky queries and spontaneous mockery.

Later he mocked the ethnographic commerce of native dream songs and creation stories as arrogant, greedy, and slanted translations of natural motion, and yet every night he mourned the atrocities of totemic animals in the fur trade and the constant deadly lure of *nisidizo*, the catch of suicide on the White Earth Reservation.

The crave of beaver hats revealed the breach of totemic unions and cultural desperation of native trappers. Colonial empires of the enlightenment plainly pardoned the massacre of totemic animals with political apologies, literary conceit, liturgical stealth, and pious reasons for the rush of fancy fur fashions. The natural totemic presence of animals, native creation stories, and healing songs were barely conceivable in heart stories after the blood wealth of beaver, marten, muskrat, otter, lynx, and other woodland peltry in three centuries of the mercenary fur trade.

La Chance created concise images as dream songs to overcome the ancestral shame for the slaughter of totemic animals, and at the same time he teased at a distance the crude native horde of deer and bear hunters rigged out in frayed camouflage costumes every autumn in the brush.

> *chorus of wolves*
> *bear totems in the white pine*
> *shouts of beaver*
> *bundled as fancy fashions*

La Chance embodied the misery, somber memory, and native shame for the slaughter of totemic animals and was mocked and bullied by students at the government school for his poetic tributes to the sound of animals and birds in natural motion, the pounce of bobcats in the snow, the dance of sandhill cranes, and the evasive bounce of blue ravens in the birch.

The government teachers tried in vain to humor the sentiments of his dream songs that honored curious totemic unions with cedar waxwings, killdeer, polyphemus moths, kingfishers, spiders, praying mantis, bats, moccasin flowers, and the consolation of reservation mongrels. He was more secure with the sound of natural motion in the willow trees and disguised his sense of abandonment with dream songs of the deceptive killdeer, dart of hummingbirds, the elusive flight of cedar waxwings, and bold maneuvers of ravens.

La Chance mocked aristocrats, bankers, politicians, cowboys, gangsters, and film noir movie actors who wore furs and costly beaver felt fedoras, and he declared at every churchy moment of repose that the poseurs of caste, colony, and culture never once honored or mourned the millions of totemic animals put to death in the colonial fur trade for a fedora or fur coat. He wrote a pithy dream song about the poseurs in fedoras.

native white pine
hewed for settlers in the cities
bankers and barons
deadly poseurs in fedoras

La Chance was silenced with the death of his parents in an automobile accident on an icy curve near Pine Point on the White Earth Reservation, Sunday, February 22, 1942, two days after his father enlisted in the army. He survived the early morning rollover and was treated for cuts and bruises by native nurses at the White Earth Hospital.

He was five years old that winter of deadly separation and carried on in silence with a wounded heart. He was denied the chance of secure names and easy stories but not the memories of his parents, the tender glances and touch of his mother, and his father dressed in a military uniform, his tease of ravens, buoyant whistles in the early morning, and double winks of devotion in the rearview mirror. The trust of heart stories and natural motion became the sounds and sources of his solace, and every day he braved the solitude of a native presence and the decoy of *nisidizo*, native suicide, and he was always ready to escape from foster homes.

Once curious with a spirited nature, he became an anxious and hesitant native fugitive and lived by chance in the creative world of totemic sounds and memories. He scarcely spoke in more than whispers and gestured to others with only two or three murmured words at a time. The haughty students at the government school mocked and teased him every day with nicknames, Beaver Breath, Tick Totem, Salt Lick, Skunk Pelt, and Chancy Murmur.

> *autumn favors*
> *elusive cedar waxwings*
> *sound of sumac*
> *totems in the clouds*

Ten years after the death of his parents, the scrawny orphan with blue eyes came to rest at the Theatre of Chance and learned how to sidetrack the snow ghosts of suicide in the silent mercy and generous teases of Dummy Trout, the miraculous mute puppeteer of Spirit Lake.

The curse of *nisidizo* started shortly after the death of his parents and became more serious in the foster homes. The ghostly echoes of suicide increased with the nicknames at the government school, and he could not overcome or escape the doubt and unease around students. Solitude and slight hesitations became an artistic manner, and he learned how to create stories and dream songs about the dignity of hesitation, sound and silence, and natural motion.

He described the slight hesitations of his speech as the unexpected silence between a flash of lightning and crash of thunder, or between the torments of memory and sudden bursts of laughter. He waited at the tree lines in summer storms for the lightening and chancy sensations of silence and fury. The solitude and hesitations became the creative source of dream songs, and later he was enchanted with the silent, gawky gestures of marvelous hand puppets at the Theatre of Chance.

La Chance counted on natural motion, the sincerity of silence and slight hesitations, as the source of wisdom and native liberty, and his resistance to hearsay traditions was necessary to overcome the lures of suicide. His sense of caution and solitude as an orphan was chancy and called for wit, courage, and resistance to endure the bullies and daily betrayals of the government school. He chose silence over sophistry and contention, hand puppets over government teachers, and quit school at age fifteen to become a native farouche and poet of concise dream songs in the marvelous company of clever mongrels and a mute puppeteer.

Dummy Trout survived a deadly firestorm in the late summer of her eighteenth birthday. She walked in circles of heartache for several days, covered her body with ashes of the native dead, and since then, she has not uttered a name, word, or song. She grieved alone through that long winter, convened the raucous ravens in the dead birch, teased the beaver, rounded up forsaken reservation mongrels, and on the snowy backroads taunted the seductive blue shadows of snow ghosts and the *wiindigoo*, a cold and vicious woodland cannibal. Nookaa, her beloved lumberjack, and hundreds of other natives and entire families were burned to bone bits and ashes and forsaken in the history of the Great Hinckley Fire of 1894.

Dummy has mourned, roared, shouted, tittered, and teased in silence for more than fifty years. She was silent and strange, a respected outsider, and cared for the spirit of children, mongrels, animals, birds, and puppets, and never shouted into panic holes. The mute puppeteer with white hair was an opera aficionado and far more memorable than most natives on the reservation. She teased mongrels with the favor of operas, cut short the curse and cruelty of bullies and federal agents with silent gestures. She never revealed sacred or given names, and never responded to the hearsay that she had chased down a fur trader in the canoe country to secure the freshwater surname Trout.

La Chance created a dream song about the great fire and the mute puppeteer of the Theatre of Chance. Churchy natives and missionaries once prayed over a rusty dented coffee canister of coarse white powder, convinced by their devotion that the paltry share of ashes came from the actual sifted bodies of dead native relatives. The Great Hinckley Fire started after a long drought on Saturday, September 1, 1894, and the firestorm destroyed at least six small towns, logging camps cluttered with slash and woodchip debris, and hundreds of thousands of acres of pine forests.

silent puppeteer
teases the spirit of natives
new dream songs in the clouds
ashes of memory

Dummy composed scenes of sorrow, the gentle shows of silence and sen-
suous enticements of suicide, the ironic episodes of puppet parleys, original
dream songs, and notes in four blank books that were shelved near a narrow
bunk along with many other books, including *American Indian Stories* by
Zitkala Sa, *Middlemarch* by George Eliot, *Wynema, A Child of the Forest*
by S. Alice Callahan, *Moby-Dick* by Herman Melville, *Walden* by Henry
Thoreau, *The Call of the Wild* by Jack London, *Animal Farm* by George
Orwell, three boxed volumes of *The Essays of Michel de Montaigne*, *The
Ghost Dance Religion and the Sioux Outbreak of 1890* published by the
Bureau of American Ethnology, and the comic novel *The History of Tom
Jones, a Foundling* by Henry Fielding.

Dummy was a serious reader, and every night by the warm wavering
light of an Aladdin Mantel Lamp she read books, out of date newspapers,
and magazines. The blank books were bound with leather and contained
selected quotations and concise notes from the books she had read. The
primary sources of the eclectic stack of books were favors from the many
visitors, politicians, ethnographers, teachers, artists, and authors who had
stayed at the Leecy Hotel on the White Earth Reservation.

books at peace
abandoned in libraries
stacked in silent rows
dead authors
come alive overnight

Dummy created dream songs in five lines, never three or four lines, and
some songs teased the cant of traditions, ruins of culture, snow ghosts, suicide, totemic unions, and others were poetic tributes to opera divas. She
once printed dream songs on note cards and presented them at afternoon
radio operas at the Leecy Hotel.

Dummy lived with four mongrels, divas Hail Mary, George Eliot,
Dingleberry, and one divo, Trophy Bay, at the Theatre of Chance, a roomy
ramshackle cabin covered with tarpaper near the shore of Spirit Lake. She
has mimed, teased, and gestured in silence the visionary presence of great
sopranos of the opera with hand puppets and loyal mongrels at her side for
more than thirty years.

Dummy wrote notes and dream songs on two chalk boards, one inside and the other on the outside of the entry door. The outside notes lasted only a few days in fair weather, and on the inside board she wrote dream songs.

silent memories
heart of natural motion
totemic secrets
massacre of the fur trade
native fear and fury

Trophy Bay, a mongrel coonhound, was ostracized for his haunting melancholy baritone bays during services and sacred recitations at the Benedictine mission. He continued to bay at a distance to torment the mission priest. Hail Mary, an elusive spaniel and husky mongrel with a clear melodic bark, pranced with the heartbeat of opera music. George Eliot, a racy greyhound and retriever mongrel, raised the hair on the arms of lonesome natives with the singular grace of her soprano moans, magical soughs, and spirited sighs. Dingleberry, a spotted black and white terrier danced in circles as she yodeled around the cabin with the arias of great sopranos of the opera.

divas chase dreams
graves of diva mongrels
bounty of melancholy
moans and bays
native theatre of chance

The Theatre of Chance was a quirky court of operatic mongrels and hand puppets, and almost everyone on the reservation remembered the first five mongrels as great singers, Papa Pius, Miinan, Queena, Makwa, and Snatch. The loyal mongrels were buried with ironic sacraments in separate grave houses near Spirit Lake. La Chance created a dream song about the operatic mongrels and the puppeteer.

dummy trout
shrouds of wild white hair
chance and cedar smoke
graves of diva mongrel

Miinan was a great blue mongrel singer with a glorious sonorous bay. Queena was a basset hound and retriever mongrel with a gentle operatic moan, and she was one of the marvelous voices of the great operas conducted by the hand puppets. The moans and bays of the operatic mongrels were more totemic and memorable than the beat, mood, and tone of singers on the noisy overnight radio road shows.

The New York Metropolitan Opera broadcast the first live performances on radio during the Great Depression, and natives and guests once gathered around a radio console to hear weekly operas at the Leecy Hotel. Queena listened to the broadcast of the soprano Queena Mario in the opera *Hansel and Gretel* and raised her golden head and bayed in perfect harmony with the opera scenes and gestures of the hand puppets.

Dummy listened to great opera divas on a Silvertone hand crank record player from Sears, Roebuck & Company and silently directed the mongrels to bay and moan with the gestures of hand puppets. Dummy had carved from fallen birch the wooden heads of the great sopranos Geraldine Farrar and Alma Gluck, and the mongrels delivered divine bays and operatic moans.

The Theatre of Chance was not connected to electrical service, and the only source of light at night was the steady glow of a flat wick Aladdin Mantel Lamp. Several times a week the unwound phonograph slowed the sound of the opera singers to moans, mumbles, and slurs, and the loyal mongrels mimicked the drowsy pitch of voices with weary and dreary moans and bays. The mongrels seemed to wait for the perfect moment to mock the voices of great opera singers.

The Theatre of Chance was a curious sanctuary for runaways. The strange stories of the mute puppeteer and operatic mongrels were more worrisome for some native fugitives than outright neglect, abuse, and desertion on the reservation. Nothing was ever the same after two world wars. The ordinary spirit, gestures, worries, and communal care of relatives were barely dependable or secure despite the charitable hearsay of native traditions. Many native runaways were abused at home and teased at school but found solace at the Theatre of Chance.

native fugitives
favored by the loyal mongrels
teased by the hand puppets
spirit lake stowaways

Truman La Chance, Big Rant Beaulieu, Master Jean Bonga, Poesy May Fairbanks, and Bad Boy Aristotle were the only runaways who endured for more than a few days the teases, diversions, and silent mockery of the mute puppeteer and the decisive slobber of the four loyal mongrels. The mongrels favored some runaways with buoyant operatic moans and sloppy chins on the thigh and slowly nosed the others, the poseurs of tradition and bullies of scorn and separation stories, out the door. The chosen runaways were regarded by the loyal mongrels as totemic stowaways at the Theatre of Chance.

Master Jean Bonga was a runaway with a historical namesake, and he arrived with Daniel, a loyal black spaniel with an ironic service name for Captain Daniel Robertson the opportunistic slaver of the fur trade who owned Jean Bonga in the late seventeen hundreds when Captain Daniel was the commander at Fort Michilimackinac.

Dummy raised and waved her hands to applaud the ironic genealogy and learned later that his mother created the ironic nickname of a monarch or slave master. Hail Mary barked and pranced with favor, and Daniel responded with a gentle bay for the first time at the Theatre of Chance.

Big Rant and Poesy May stayed in the main cabin with Dummy Trout, La Chance, Bad Boy, and Master Jean were consigned to the smaller cabin nearby. The stowaways came together with a similar sense of natural motion, sounds and heart stories. They concocted two meals a day, breakfast was always oatmeal and thick maple syrup that had been tapped in the spring, and dinner was a mound of beans and wild rice, bass, crappie, and northern pike from the lake, and in summer, vegetables from the garden, and every morning fresh eggs from more than a dozen loyal chickens in the lath house or those that nested under the two cabins. Sources of food were always a desperate game of chance in the winter, and the poseurs of native traditions who mainly hunted for bear and deer hardly ever returned with more than an exaggerated overnight story. There were a few natives with agency connections who never missed a meal of salt pork and commodity cheese.

Families on the reservation were starving in winter and sometimes in the summer, and the only daily meal for many children was at the government and mission day schools, but some children were too cold and hungry in the winter to even get out of bed. Students at the Saint Benedict Mission

Boarding School were once the most secure, but the mission school closed at the end of the Second World War.

Joseph Edward Vizenor, the elected vice president of the Minnesota Chippewa Tribe, and other natives met with Senator Hubert Humphrey and Governor Luther Youngdahl to report that thousands of natives were facing starvation on many reservations in Minnesota. The Commodity Credit Corporation had surplus potatoes, apples, dried skim milk, eggs, honey, and other food in storage, but hungry natives were told that not enough trucks were available to deliver the surplus food to reservations.

The Soo Line Railroad constructed stations at Ogema, Callaway, and Mahnomen more than forty years ago on the White Earth Reservation. The stations became an enticement to those who exploited native resources. Hordes of hunters traveled by train and decimated moose, deer, bear, and other animals on the reservation. The timber barons destroyed the natural wild rice on lakes and rivers, and then metropolitan mercenaries hunted down the last animals that provided food for natives.

The Great Depression caused many natives to move from the desperation and hunger on treaty reservations to Minneapolis, and some natives were active in the Truckers' Strike. The same union of truckers might have remembered the past and delivered food to hungry natives.

hungry children
wait near the white pine stumps
potatoes and evaporated milk
stacked out of reach
marketeers lost their way

Dummy never counted on governments for anything, not for fatty federal pork from a barrel or the metes and bounds of an obscure land allotment on the reservation. She compared the constant poses and promises of federal agents to the most wicked turns of hearsay. The silence of natives always distracted the insecure federal agents and haunted the priests, but the lively hand puppet parleys never failed to charm most natives. Dummy and the mongrels and stowaways were always at ease at the Theatre of Chance.

2

LITERARY MERCY

Bad Boy Aristotle, Big Rant Beaulieu, Poesy May Fairbanks, Master Jean Bonga, Bunker Boy Beaulieu, and Kristian Lars Hokkanen, the fleshy Finnish boy who lived on a nearby farm, were the only students who salvaged burned books from the fire debris of the Library of Nibwaakaa, the library of the wise and clever on the White Earth Reservation.

Bad Boy used a garden shovel to rescue smoldering plays by William Shakespeare, *Hamlet, The Merchant of Venice, King Lear, Romeo and Juliet,* a badly scorched copy of *Poetics* by Aristotle, and *The Essays of Michel de Montaigne. The Complete Greek Drama* edited by Whitney Oats and Eugene O'Neill was badly burned and demanded great imagination.

Big Rant, the marvelous reader, winnowed the dark ashes and uncovered partly burned copies of *Moby-Dick* by Herman Melville, *The Adventures of Tom Sawyer* by Mark Twain, *Light in August* by William Faulkner, *Look Homeward, Angel* by Thomas Wolfe, *For Whom the Bell Tolls* by Ernest Hemingway, and *The Catcher in the Rye* by J. D. Salinger.

Poesy May pranced through the ashes and found six burned books of poetry, *A Further Range* and *A Witness Tree* by Robert Frost, *The Complete Poetical Works of John Keats, The People, Yes* by Carl Sandburg, *Leaves of Grass* and *Drum-Taps* by Walt Whitman. She read poetry in whispers and created a sense of solace in muted poetic soughs and sighs.

Master Jean plowed through the ashes of the library and rescued *The Voyageur* and *Caesars of the Wilderness* by Grace Lee Nute, *History of the Ojibway People* by William Warren, *Hiroshima* by John Hersey, and *Grapes of Wrath* by John Steinbeck.

Bunker Boy slowly raked through the ruins of the library for cowboy stories and recovered four novels, *The Virginian* by Owen Wister, *Riders of the Purple Sage* by Zane Grey, *The Log of a Cowboy* by Andy Adams, and *The Ox-Bow Incident* by Walter Van Tilburg Clark.

Kristian Lars found three slightly scorched volumes of the fourteenth edition of the *Encyclopedia Britannica.* At age thirteen he set out to read every entry in the twenty-three volumes and index of the *Britannica* and had read about a hundred pages of the first volume, *A to Annoy,* when an arsonist destroyed the Library of Nibwaakaa. He shouted out with delight three times and raised volumes twelve, fifteen and nineteen from the ashes. Later he told the others that he had already read the entry for the Library of Alexandria.

Bad Boy Aristotle arrived at dusk one summer night with bruises on his cheeks, arms, and shoulders and, with no introduction, read out loud short selections from one of the burned books he carried in a backpack. Bad Boy read from the burned pages and created the content and scenes of the absent words on the margins. He countered the piety of grammar, turned shadows of burned words into good cheer, and easily grasped the native wont of creation stories and literary mercy at the Theatre of Chance.

"Creation stories are in the clouds and on the pages of burned books," shouted Bad Boy. He was small with thin bones, gentle, and hardly built for even the slightest body blows. "The burned words are envoys of natural motion and ready to be created as dream songs, teases on the run, and heard far and wide."

A few days later he was favored by the mongrels, and only then he told hesitant stories about a violent uncle, a pulp cutter and cheap whiskey drunkard. Bad Boy was beaten once or twice a week because the chesty boozer despised his abandoned nephew, cursed him as a weakling, and hated the smell of burned books as much as he hated the faint scent of school rooms and the Library of Nibwaakaa.

"No classical tragedy in my stories," Bad Boy insisted that night at the Theatre of Chance. "No tragic play of words or regrets because violence on the reservation is our story, always our story, and sometimes disguised as a down and out treaty trick, but the nicknames, shuns, curses, and cruelty that natives bear is workaday."

Bad Boy carried a burned copy of *Poetics* by Aristotle, one volume of *The Essays of Michel de Montaigne,* and other books from the ruins of the library. He learned to read and respect the world views of philosophy not only from the center or heart of the burned books but from the very scenes he created on the margins of burned pages. He created memorable native scenes from the ashes of the library.

Bad Boy read out loud the printed centers and at the same time created another version of the burned pages of *Poetics* that night at the Theatre of Chance. He imagined with no hesitation scenes of natural motion from the burned ashes of the book, and related stories about classical tragedy and the imitation of totemic animals.

A native dream song *seems to have sprung from two causes* and the sense of natural motion was the *instinct of imitation* in trickster stories, and almost the *difference between him and other animals.* Totemic animals are the *most imitative of living creatures.* A dream song is *one instinct of our nature,* and the native tease *is the instinct for harmony,* and trickster creation stories of stones and relations *started with this natural gift* of the great flood, an urge to crap, and tease the totemic service of beaver and muskrats.

Trickster stories *diverged in two directions,* and totemic animal *spirits imitated noble actions,* and the actions of a wise trickster and the good shamans *imitated the actions of meaner persons* with deceptive sounds. The outcome of native tragedy is *an imitation of action that is serious,* and natives created origin stories that were *embellished with each kind of artistic ornament* as the necessary versions of a once great totemic culture before the deceptive discoveries and the dreadful continental fur trade.

Big Rant Beaulieu was abandoned as a newborn child at the old mission. She was covered with a remnant of black velvet in a birch bark basket. The deserted child was named Ellanora Mary Beaulieu to honor the memory of the native military nurse who died of influenza at the end of the First World War.

Big Rant was a rapid reader, and she read out loud books, newspapers, letters, highway signs, names, and advertisements with no hesitation, every printed word was out loud. The notes between students were never silent or secret at the mission boarding school or at the day school. No teases, catty names, censure, or intended humiliation distracted the tiny native with huge black eyes from her ordinary broadcast of every printed word in range of her vision.

Big Rant was a raven on the wind, a raven in the birch, a clever raven in the brush, and she perceived natural motion and the tease of liberty. The nuns praised her enthusiasm, impressive range of vocabulary, and bold manner of pronunciation, but no one could quiet the most incredible reader on the reservation. No one could easily quiet a raven.

Big Rant read out loud with no trace of uncertainty or shy poses. Her voice was clear, perfectly pitched, and she was never silent with a book in hand. Her only hesitations as a reader were the absence of some printed words in books, the books burned in the fire at the Library of Nibwaakaa. The sound of her steady voice was weakened to mere mumbles over the burned pages, and with pauses she created uneasy sentences.

Big Rant created scenes from the burned page of the novel *Moby-Dick* by Herman Melville that summer at the Theatre of Chance. Hail Mary and George Eliot had already slobbered on her sleeve, the foremost gesture of acceptance as a stowaway of Spirit Lake. The mongrels moaned and faintly barked when they heard the slight pauses and tone of voice in the scenes about watery parts and coffin warehouses.

Call me Ellanora Mary. *Some years ago*, since the time of burned books, *having little or no money*, and only dream songs to *interest me on shore*, we paddled fur trade canoes in the *watery parts of the world*, and with trickster creation stories for *regulating the circulation* of totemic animals and disease, *growing grim about the mouth*, and distracted by the wicked winter *in my soul, whenever I find myself* looking for my native friends at *coffin warehouses, and bringing up* the last bundles of animals in the mercenary fur trade. There is always time, *especially whenever my hypos* or shame and cultural disgrace for the slaughter of totemic animals and demise of native creation stories *requires a strong moral principle*, or the courage to denounce the fakery of native traditions and create original totemic stories before *stepping into the street* at night to resist the enterprise of timber barons and the deceit of federal agents.

Master Jean created scenes from the badly burned pages of *The Voyageur* by Grace Lee Nute. He was never secure reading out loud, but that night in the good company of the mongrels and stowaways the delivery of burned scenes was much easier to whisper and shout. The cover and pages of the book were badly burned on three margins, and every page of *The Voyageur* was browned from the heat of the library fire.

My man dressed in the strange clothes of the enemy of totemic animals, *a short shirt, a red woolen* fedora and a crude blowsy costume with *leggins which from the ankles* to his bony knees are *held up by a string* tied around his dirty neck, and around *the waist* a simulated native breechclout and a *pair of deer skin moccasins* formed to his bare feet. *The thighs are left bare* and warns everyone he is a *voyageur in summer and winter*. And remember *the worthy missionary, Sherman Hall* who was aroused by *a blue capote, the inevitable pipe* and who knows what he carries in *a gay beaded bag or pouch hung* over the puckers of his chest, *and you have the voyageur as he appeared* half dressed and ready to thrust a short paddle over *lakes, advancing cautiously up narrow creeks* to *portages, cracking his whip over the heads* of dead animals of the fur trade, and *laughing down rapids, fiddling in log forts* to the end of the natural world. *One would expect voyageurs to be men*, but they were nothing more than the outcasts of nature, *five feet six inches in height*, and some might *stand five foot eight*, and as the wild *voyageur was short, he was strong*, but crude and heartless, and he could paddle for *weeks on end and joke* about native women on the trail and make merry the massacre of millions of beaver and totemic animals overnight around a campfire.

Dummy raised her arms over her head, smiled, waved her hands, wagged her fingers, and shouted brava, brava, brava in silence to celebrate the creative renditions of burned pages by the stowaways. Daniel, the black spaniel newcomer at the Theatre of Chance, bounced on his front paws, and the other four mongrels bayed and soughed over the good cheer of the stowaways. Dummy printed an original dream song on the inside chalk board.

> *native stowaways*
> *saved a library of burned books*
> *ashes of words in motion*
> *created ironic scenes*
> *lasting dream songs of liberty*

Dummy printed a quotation by Michel de Montaigne on the chalk board at the end of the dream song. Two or three times a week she read essays of the philosopher in translation, and copied selected quotations in notebooks, but that evening was the first time that she noted his ideas along with a dream song on the chalk board. Montaigne reads "to become more wise, not more learned or eloquent," she wrote, and "the world knows me in my book, and my book is me."

Bad Boy Aristotle, Big Rant Beaulieu, and Master Jean created native scenes of natural motion from the ashes of the burned books. Dummy and the stowaways never created new scenes from the burned pages of *The Essays of Michel de Montaigne.*

3

ROYAL LIBERTY

Master Jean Bonga carved the natural curve of a bow from green ash and hewed seven arrows from a juneberry bush that summer when his frail mother was diagnosed with tuberculosis and calmly carried away to the Ahgwahching State Sanatorium on Shingobee Bay near the Leech Lake Reservation.

He waited alone in silence. Another day, another night he waited on the uneven stoop, only a month away from his sixth birthday, and late one night he raised the dented bugle that his father had inherited and played a few notes of the Last Post.

Alone for more than five days, the lonesome heir of the fur trade gathered the wood chips on the stoop, a natural gesture to please his mother, and then waited to hear the gentle sound of her melodious voice. A week later he marched to the post office and listened to stories and hearsay.

Nagamo Trotterchaud, his tiny mother, was born in a cold wigwam on the Ash River Trail near Sullivan Bay. The family was always hungry, and she was the only one of three children who survived the winters of despair and poverty. Her native mother was stranded in misery with a headstrong *coureur de bois* of the bygone fur trade.

Nagamo met George Bonga at a Métis summer gathering and they were married a few months later at the White Earth Reservation. She was weakened by the birth of Jean and never fully recovered from the long delivery, and never said a word about the years of fatigue, chest pain, fever, and other symptoms of tuberculosis.

George enlisted in the military five years later and served in a segregated transportation company as a daring truck driver for the Red Ball Express in the Second World War. Nagamo worked a few days a week at the government school and never earned enough money to support the family. She was grateful for the slightest pleasures of a balmy summer day, and always praised the pluck and vigor of her son Jean. She wrote to her husband once a week but never revealed the diagnosis of tuberculosis or the Ahgwahch-ing State Sanatorium.

Master Jean cut traditional scallops on the sides of the bow, finished the arrows with chicken feathers and crude metal points, and a month later he crouched in the brush and waited in silent misery to sacrifice animals or birds near Spirit Lake.

The short bow was not strong enough to down a deer, or even disable a fox or curious bobcat, and the gray squirrels were out of reach, wary as the ravens circled and warned about the presence of the enemy. The clumsy scene of vengeance was solemn and pathetic, and on the second morning the lonesome hunter was distracted by a deserted and hungry black spaniel. The dedicated preparations of the hunt were easily set aside in the eager company of a reservation mongrel.

Master Jean never sacrificed an animal or bird in silent rage, and never again blamed the breach of totemic relations for his misery. He converted his torment, loneliness, and grievances to concentrate on the art of archery. A few months later the target scenes were the snow ghosts of native suicide, the elusive enemies of chance and natural motion. Luckily, the outcome of his native practice of visionary archery was an aesthetic turn to natural motion and ironic stories rather than misery, resentment, and vengeance to ease his sense of sorrow.

Master Jean became a truant only a few days after he had been admit-ted to the first grade at the Saint Benedict Mission Boarding School. His mother was confined to a sanatorium for consumptives, his native grand-mother was disabled with cancer and could not care for her grandson, and his father was a soldier in the Second World War.

The boarding school students cautiously teased the truant archer, partly out of envy for his adventures. The nicknames that first year were casual and bearable, almost tentative teases of his stature and sway, Chancy Jean, Stilts, Straight Arrow, Highbrow, Jack Pine, and Crazy Bow. Master Jean was an ironic nickname created by his mother who gently teased that he must become a native master of chance over destiny.

Master Jean was the tallest student in the first three grades of the mission school and "the notable heir of a liberated slave in the ancient fur trade," he boasted. The older students contested his racial fur trade pride and declared that he was wide of any nobility, but he was clearly a forsaken hunter with curly black hair.

Jean Bonga, the slave by way of Jamaica and the French West Indies, was owned by Captain Daniel Robertson, the military commander of the British fur trade post at Fort Michilimackinac. Jean and other slaves in the early fur trade were liberated with the death of the officer. Jean inherited a cache of peltry, a beaver hat, a dented bugle, and continued his service in the fur trade with his son Pierre who later served the prominent Alexander Henry of the Beaver Club and the North West Company. Pierre married a native, and his son George Bonga was educated in Montreal and was hired as a translator by Governor Lewis Cass. George Bonga, the second namesake, married Nagamo and their son Master Jean was a student at the Saint Benedict Mission Boarding School.

Master Jean learned to play the bugle and was determined to carry on the tradition of the five note tones of bugle calls. Captain Daniel Robertson obtained the army bugle from a veteran soldier in the fur trade and taught his slave Jean Bonga to play the Last Post at Fort Michilimackinac.

"Liberty is my royalty," declared George Bonga at least once a week, and he continued that sentiment even after his service in a segregated military company during the Second World War. He countered racial exclusions with stories about tricksters, the slights of shamans, and dreamers in the *Midewiwin* or Grand Medicine Society. He resolved that "the necessary union of humans and animals, and sometimes birds, even after the deadly fur trade was more worthy and responsible than shame, remorse, pity, or revenge." His son embraced a similar sense of natural motion, the sounds of a totemic presence, and integrity despite the atrocities of the fur trade and the ruins of civilization.

Master Jean and Daniel, the black spaniel, were royal and free by chance and always together, but the mongrel dog was not allowed in the mission school dormitory. Daniel was an ironic namesake of the military commander at Fort Michilimackinac. The loyal mongrel waited at the school door for several days until a lenient priest created a special shelter in the nearby mission barn. The priest also created straw targets for standard archery practice because he was convinced that the distant heir of a fur trade slave could with practice become a master archer.

The Minnesota State Archery Association was started a few years before

Master Jean arrived at the mission school, and the priest was eager to coach the native bowyer to compete in state archery tournaments. Several other students practiced in the barn, but the plucky native was bored with stationary targets and insisted on targets in motion. He suspended the straw targets from the rafters, concentrated on the natural motion, and almost every arrow he released hit the target. The priest could not persuade him to do the same with stationary targets, and that resistance in favor of natural motion ended the formal practice sessions with the priest.

Master Jean had already created his own bow and arrows and was conscious of a distinctive native style of archery. The easy poise of the draw, anchor point, and a visionary sense of target scenes in natural motion was in the blood, not in the usual conventions of practice or competition with a coterie of student archers.

The Saint Benedict Mission Boarding School was no longer supported by the federal agent on the reservation and closed at the end of the Second World War. Most of the students continued in the mission day school. Master Jean evaded the gestures of fosterage and pretended that he had a home. The day school students were much feistier, and he almost lost the easy sway of resistance stories that he told in the dormitory. Once more he was stranded, but with a greater sense of native presence and stay. He lived with Daniel that summer and autumn in an abandoned station wagon near the Library of Nibwaakaa.

The Theatre of Chance was a totemic union of native stories and creative hearsay, and always a place of dream songs and liberty, but the notion of chance, or even a tricky venture, was shunned in the parochial courses of study. Godly obedience and customary chores were the necessary conditions of enlightenment and salvation at the mission school. Yet, a native sense of natural motion and chance resisted the vague demons of churchy shame, and some students mocked the divine courses of colonial crafts, sewing, farming, and machinery. He learned to smile and duck the ritual prayers of redemption and sidestepped the lonesome daily count of genuflects.

Master Jean heard post office hearsay and other fantastic stories about the mute puppeteer and mongrels of the opera. The older students at the mission day school told stories that the scary mute turned children into hand puppets, and even scarier stories that the mute had turned truant students into mongrels to chase down wolves, rabbits, skunks, and a few priests.

Trophy Bay was named as the most recent mission student that the mute puppeteer had turned into a mongrel, and with a great bay. The churchy elders warned that the association with totemic animals was idolatry, and never a course of salvation with Dummy Trout and the mongrels at the Theatre of Chance.

Master Jean could no longer carry out his tricky surveys in the mission dormitory. During the final days of the mission boarding school, he asked students in the dormitory to name the books that totemic animals would likely read that year, and then he printed selected responses early one morning on the chalk board in the classroom. A few students dared to smirk and titter as the parochial teacher slowly erased the names of animals and then the references. "Bears read novels about mountain men," was erased. "Moose read stories about art museums," was erased along with "wolves read adventure comic books, river otters read poetry, mink and muskrats were dedicated readers about mission schools, and reservation mongrels read novels by Jack London."

The massacre of totemic animals was carried out in three centuries of the fur trade, and the deadly sentiments continued in monotheistic scriptures at the mission school and the derogatory scenes and similes of animals in popular literature.

The Theatre of Chance stowaways shared a buoyant sense of presence with mongrels and easily turned back with heart stories and mockery the count of greedy fur traders, the stumps of wicked timber barons, and the distorted national notion of an enlightened human dominance over natives on treaty reservations.

Dummy Trout, the hand puppets, mongrels of the opera, and stowaways have endured with stories of totemic animals, chance, and liberty over salvation and the doom and gloom of monotheism at the mission school. The Theatre of Chance encouraged creative stories of native totemic relations and circles of liberty, the same native associations and scenes of chance that preceded by thousands of years the sacred testaments, covenants, and torments of monotheism. The native spirit of chance and heart stories eluded the course of destiny and redemption with creative scenes of resistance, trickster contradictions of creation, and a sense of native presence and liberty that outlasted the churchy missions on the reservation.

Dummy created hand puppets with the clever gestures of chance over destiny, adventure over the debris of culture, and the native spirit of liberty enchanted the mongrels and stowaways.

Master Jean was the first stowaway who arrived with a mongrel, and he revealed in silence a sense of chance and natural motion in archery. He first met the other students who became stowaways at the ruins of the Library of Nibwaakaa.

Master Jean played a creative version of the Last Post on the bugle as the students waded in the ashes for the chance to rescue burned books, novels, collections of poetry, encyclopedias, classical philosophy, and with no fret or favor of competition. The students had once searched the library shelves for surprises, a distinctive author, original stories, and the adventures of a poem or novel, but to find a burned book in the ruins was a much greater wonder because the burned margin of the pages waited to be created by another author and the chance of an original native adventure of literary liberty.

4

SNOW GHOSTS

Bunker Boy Beaulieu was more at ease as an outrider or solitary swing man in cowboy stories than as a student of social studies, grammar, science, mathematics, or the bogus chronicles of custody cultures at the government school.

He would rather read *The Log of a Cowboy* by Andy Adams and picture that lively morning, April 1, 1882, when the "Circle Dot herd started on its long tramp to the Blackfoot Agency in Montana," and with "six men on each side, and the herd strung out for three quarters of a mile, it could be compared to some mythical serpent." The "herd trailed along behind the leaders like an army in loose marching order, guarded by outriders, known as the swing men, who rode well out from the advancing column."

Seventy years later, April 1, 1952, on a cold spring morning, the literary outrider and solitary student hanged himself from a crossbeam in a stable near the ruins of the Library of Nibwaakaa. The native police reported that a wide leather belt was hitched around the blue neck of Bunker Boy Beaulieu.

He was almost an orphan, almost anonymous in the ruins of native culture, in the same way as so many other native children who never quite related to an actual father. The overnight count of mutable men with his mother was never an ordinary touch of paternity or family. He was alone with only wispy shadows and traces of snow ghosts that seduce lonesome natives to rest forever on a cold night or bear the winter lures in any season of suicide.

Bunker died with the prominent surname of a fugitive father and created relations from the steady gloats and manly stories of men he overheard at night, but the easygoing characters in the cowboy novels he read at the library were more sincere adventures and lasting memories.

Bunker was an eager reader and praised by the librarian at the Library of Nibwaakaa. The cracked leather chair near the back window of the library became a saddle, and once or twice a week he mounted a spotted Appaloosa, and with other outriders in the cowboy novels cantered over the plains and deserts with a sense of eternal presence and native liberty. His summer mounts were envisioned only at the library before the books were burned to ashes.

Harmony Baswewe, the librarian, related the spectacular adventures of her great native uncle Luster Browne, the Baron of Patronia, who shouted his torment and outrage into panic holes and provoked other natives to shout into the earth to banish misery, mourn the abuse of totemic animals, and to perceive a sense of native presence and liberty. Sorrows of the heart were buried with shouts, and the shouts were more than confessions of shame, separation, or the weary words of cultural casualties.

Natives who never shouted into space, place, or hollows and who never praised the masters of mockery became the slaves of absolution and risky hope on the dry runs to salvation. Luster Browne shouted into panic holes for wonder, nerve, irony, and good cheer on a natural meadow near the Theatre of Chance.

Bunker was never buoyed to shout, and he never found a panic hole in the right season. Suicide was his confession about nothing to the snow ghosts, only a sense of absence and misery with the godly cast of hope and shame. He was easy prey for hearsay, hokey slipstream traditions, and sorrow as a lonesome native with no totemic tease of nature or resistance to mockery and wicked nicknames. The outrider never seemed to grasp the overtures of satire, the irony of saddle sores from a leather chair at the library, the rescue of burned cowboy books, or that fanciful herd of animals on the long mercenary tramp to slaughterhouses.

The solitary outrider erected snow bunkers under the white pine, and two or three times every winter, he was seduced by the blue shadows of the snow ghosts to rest and sleep and almost suffocated when he waited overnight for the bunker dome to collapse in a snowstorm.

Carmen Bear was cast as a mean mutable mother at the Theatre of Chance. She carried out the feigned devotions of maternity no more than once a week and grazed in cut and run native traditions, cosmetic obsessions, overnight promises, and at the same time, she gulped cheap red wine and courted nightly roamers for attention. She never earned a native sense of time or temper and was named an easy pushover in reservation stories.

Prosper Makwa, her father, was named in honor of Prosper Mérimée,

author of the novel *Carmen*, because his father was obsessed with the popular story, especially the scenes of Don José, who deserted the cavalry for
passion, jealousy, and the sensational conversion and execution of Carmen
in the opera by Georges Bizet. Prosper merged and enhanced the scenes of
the novel and the opera with every version of the story he told at the post
office, hotel lobbies, and government school.

Prosper named his first daughter Carmen to continue the curious tradition of operatic names in the family. His son, who died at age five, was
named Bizet Makwa. Carmen Bear resisted the native surname, and she
could not carry a tune or show any pleasure of opera music, but she was
lusty and contentious and the constant theme of reservation hearsay. Carmen roused more erotic teases and taunts than any other native student at
the old government school, and in that spirited way she conveyed the operatic traditions of the family names.

Carmen Bear was a poseur in a blond wig who craved fatty foods and
heartlessly shamed her son Bunker Boy as thick and fleshy. The lonesome
cowboy longed for steady casual care and devotion, and she served him
crackers and salty chunks of pork belly from a barrel. Healthier meals were
provided once a day at the government school, but he could hardly bear to
run the gauntlet of the bullies and nicknames, Little Big Belly, Snow Drift,
Bunker Brain, and Cowboy Boner, to eat chewy poultry, mushy beans, de-
hydrated potatoes, commodity cheese, and canned fruit.

Dummy Trout stared down the snow ghosts every winter, and she roused
others with silent teases to outplay the seductive demons of separation and
the deceptions of hope and suicide. She mourned in silence over the desolation and cultural murder of children, and that prompted the federal agent
to report with unintended irony, "The Dummy ramshackle cabin near
Spirit Lake is a resistance school for runaway readers, dopey hand puppets,
reservation mongrels, and tricky combat with student suicides."

Big Rant Beaulieu read out loud the dream song and notes that Dummy
had written in a blank book about the suicide of Bunker Boy. Big Rant and
Bunker Boy could have been related to native newspaper editors, a photog-
rapher, army combat veterans, or a musician with the same surname, but
their actual fathers were never revealed.

"Bunker Boy lost his sense of native chance and was enticed by the snow ghosts and sacrificed on a risky road of deliverance. Reservations are tragic operas of suicide, and he was never teased enough to learn the creative comebacks with a better story than the leftovers of grace and the churchy gibberish of hope, shame, and destiny. Solace in the Library of Nibwaakaa and the characters he courted in cowboy novels were his brave delusions of liberty."

> *snow ghosts*
> *lures of hope and liberty*
> *murder the name*
> *twice the mockery and shame*
> *overnight outrider*

Bunker Boy was an outrider weakened and silenced by the destruction of the library, and the rescue of loyal characters in cowboy novels was not enough to counter the snow ghosts and mockery of nicknames at the government school. Hail Mary and Trophy Bay would have favored the stout outrider with slobbers and tender bays.

The Theatre of Chance was a crucial refuge for runaways, and the bright diversions of puppetry and mockery countered the deceptions of governments, converted the missions, outpaced the arithmetic of federal blood quantum, double teased the timber barons, priests, pagans, pulp cutters, pretended to revise treaties, and overturned with ironic stories the treachery of federal agents.

Native suicides could have been created as tragic operas with a lively cruise of mockery, the glint of soprano snow ghosts, contests of cultural separation, and moody hope of destiny as the outliers of cultural resistance. The actual suicides of native sons, daughters, and orphans on reservations were familiar stories of misery, deception, and shame, and more monstrous than the staged entertainment of suicides in the world history of opera.

The ambiguous librettos of reservation operas revealed the betrayals of integrity, character, and native liberty, and the catch of lonesome children in the ruins of civilization were deserted at government and mission schools and tormented with contrived traditions and custody cultures.

hand puppets
scare the snow ghosts
curves of memory
shame and suicide
scenes of native mockery

Dummy carved a new hand puppet later that week and the chubby face and sturdy thick hands that emerged from the rough block of fallen birch was a miniature resemblance of Bunker Boy Beaulieu. The pudgy puppet wore chaps and a white cowboy hat cocked back on his head. The memorial puppet held in one hand a miniature novel entitled *The Log of a Cowboy* by Andy Adams.

Dummy hooked a chalk board on the outside of the door and printed concise messages that lasted for two or three days in good weather. The mongrels raised their heads as the chalk squeaked on the board, and yesterday she printed, "Make hand puppets to muck up the snow ghosts and suicide. Big show at cemetery for Bunker Boy."

Poesy May Fairbanks compared the snow ghosts to the transparent snow domes or glitter globes and concocted a similar scene with a Mason jar filled with water and white glitter, the mundane simulation of a snow ghost globe that was hardly seductive. The glitter and glints were whispers of mockery.

bunker boy
overturned the snow ghosts
captured with glitter in a mason jar
solemn showdown
cowboy rides out of the stable

The Mason jar was an ironic gesture and evoked the necessary stories that slight the temptation of snow ghosts as nothing more than an upended everyday jar of glitter. George Eliot, the mongrel greyhound, rendered a soprano moan that raised the hair on the arms of the onlookers at the cemetery every time the snow ghost globe was overturned.

Big Rant Beaulieu created a puppet hunter of snow ghosts from a badly burned gazetteer in the ruins of the library. The oversized book was rounded and distorted by the fire, and the cover was an ashen image of the earth with bright red eyes and the wide mouth of a predator painted with dark red nail polish. She fastened a stick to the back of the predator of snow ghosts and fashioned a black cape from a remnant of velvet.

Big Rant raised the hunter gazetteer on her right hand and pages of crumpled newspaper as the snow ghost in her left hand. She rehearsed the voice of the gazetteer in loud authentic tones and announced the newspaper caricature of the snow ghost in a softer, more seductive tone of voice.

> GAZETTEER: Banished forever the snow ghosts.
>
> SNOW GHOST: Native hope, shame, and suicide.
>
> GAZETTEER: The seasons are never godly shame.
>
> SNOW GHOST: Snow ghosts are envoys of suicide.
>
> GAZETTEER: Deadly envoys around the world.
>
> SNOW GHOST: Natives are easily lured to suicide.
>
> GAZETTEER: Only deceptions to blame for suicide.
>
> SNOW GHOST: Suicides are not badly burned books.
>
> GAZETTEER: Snow ghosts fear the heart of books.
>
> SNOW GHOST: Authors are the ghosts in libraries.
>
> GAZETTEER: Mockery melts away the snow ghosts.

Truman La Chance created a spectacular catcher of snow ghosts with a huge white glove, and on each finger the names of five native warriors were printed in bold black print, Geronimo, Hole in the Day, Sitting Bull, Crazy Horse, and Chief Joseph on the thumb of the glove. The warriors were mustered to defeat the snow ghosts with wise sayings, or at last the essential tease of resistance. La Chance intended to carry out the voices of the five warriors to catch the seductive snow ghosts at the cemetery, but the books with the actual quotations of the warriors were burned and undiscovered in the ashes of the Library of Nibwaakaa.

Bad Boy Aristotle created a hideous demon with a rusted Maxwell House coffee tin and huge coat buttons as black eyes that haunted the snow ghosts and condemned seducers to death in a small funeral pyre near the Beaulieu Family Monument in Saint Benedict's Catholic Cemetery.

The Maxwell House hand puppet exposed the elusive snow ghosts as secret agents of colonial governments enlisted to seduce natives on reservations with racy suicide stories. Bad Boy slowly raised the demon on his right hand, and the coffee tin puppet denounced the snow ghosts disguised as pure white pompoms, and one by one the demon sentenced the suicide agents to death in a snow ghost pyre.

Bad Boy was the voice of the demon, and Big Rant practiced a lusty whisper for the voice of the pompom snow ghosts. The mongrels cocked their heads and bayed with the words of the demon, and Dingleberry yodeled and danced in circles around the funeral pyre.

Dummy directed the spring puppet parley and Big Rant rehearsed the lines for the new Bunker Boy puppet show at the cemetery. Big Rant was Cinderella, the hesitant and seductive falsetto voice of the snow ghost, and La Chance was the voice of Bunker Boy. The tribute was personal, blunt, and ironic in the elusive manner of the mute puppeteer, and only the most charitable missionaries would bear witness to a strange snow ghost and suicide puppet parley.

Dummy raised Bunker Boy the puppet on her right hand, moved his head down and to the side, a shy gesture, and on the other hand she raised a Little Darling Cinderella Doll dressed in a tattered white evening gown as the snow ghost of suicide.

Trophy Bay, the mongrel coonhound, raised his head and delivered a mellow melancholy baritone bay with the words of Bunker Boy. The bay was all the more emotive that afternoon because the mongrel had been banished from the mission and services at the cemetery for his marvelous baritone bay. Hail Mary, the spaniel and husky mongrel, presented a spirited melodic bark and at the same time she turned and swayed with the motion of the snow ghost Little Darling Cinderella Doll.

CINDERELLA: Hanged at last from a belt in a stable.
BUNKER BOY: Almost smothered in a snow bunker.
CINDERELLA: Hope shows the easy way to suicide.
BUNKER BOY: Hope was always on my mind.
CINDERELLA: Snow seductions, not horse stables.
BUNKER BOY: Treaty reservations are native stables.
CINDERELLA: Snowy nights are romantic operas.
BUNKER BOY: Your voice overcomes nasty teases.
CINDERELLA: Come to me with hope and misery.
BUNKER BOY: Lonely characters of hope and shame.
CINDERELLA: Come sleep with me in the snow.

BUNKER BOY: My snow bunkers were built for you.

CINDERELLA: Shy native cowboy of eternal shame.

BUNKER BOY: Rescued from three winter bunkers.

CINDERELLA: Teases of ransom for more than one.

BUNKER BOY: Saved my neck was the mockery.

CINDERELLA: Better to build weaker snow bunkers.

BUNKER BOY: Promise of snow ghosts in a stable.

CINDERELLA: Native cowboys ride horses of hope.

BUNKER BOY: My saddle burned with the library.

CINDERELLA: Snow ghosts are never cowboys.

BUNKER BOY: Pray for me as the cowboy of hope.

CINDERELLA: Outriders of hope are easy to seduce.

Three pious acolytes of the nearby mission observed the puppet parley at a distance and remained detached to avoid the suicide back talk of hand puppets and the seductive primal moans of the mongrels. They carried out once more customary shuns of native mockery. The missionaries prayed in silence that suicide was a mortal sin, not a talky hand puppet, and the churchy spectacle of the body was owned in monotheistic creation stories. No dream songs, native reveals, mockeries, or ironic puppet parleys would convince the righteous mission scouts that native suicide stories were not blasphemy. Native suicide was the absence of irony and maybe the confessions of churchy shame, but not a curse or sacrilege.

The King James Bible must have survived the fire at the Library of Nibwaakaa. No one ever found a burned copy in the ruins, but all the same, with even a slightly burned copy of the Holy Scriptures in hand Truman La Chance, Big Rant Beaulieu, and Bad Boy Aristotle would have created a more winsome sense of native presence, chance, and liberty at the Theatre of Chance. Puppets would be saluted as obvious trickster spirits, mongrels would become healers, martyrs would be honored with mockery, hope, shame, and separation. Suicide would be reversed with the mercy of native teases, ridicule, and ironic native stories. The overstated biblical commandment, "Thou shalt not kill" would never again betray the presence of totemic animals or excuse the mercenary fur trade in the burned pages of the new scriptures at the Theatre of Chance.

Trophy Bay, the mongrel coonhound, was exiled from the mission and cemetery because of his poignant baritone bay at services, and puppet parleys about native chance, snow ghosts, and the mockery of hope and suicide were rightly condemned as ungodly, yet the priest and churchy censors scarcely mention the great operas that celebrate suicide as tragic entertainment.

5

Madama Butterfly

Dummy Trout printed a notice on the outside chalk board that the soprano aria "Un bel dì, vedremo" of *Madama Butterfly* by Giacomo Puccini would be performed after dark at the Theatre of Chance. She created two new dream songs about the opera and copied phrases of the aria on note cards for the stowaways. The mongrels raised their wet noses and were ready to bay, moan, and bark with the recorded opera performance.

geisha butterfly
renounced traditions for love
married a cocky american lieutenant
waited three years with her son
betrayed by a naval officer

La Chance, Big Rant, Bad Boy, Master Jean, and Poesy May Fairbanks waited side by side with the mongrels to hear the great Japanese soprano Tamaki Miura sing the most famous aria "Un bel dì, vedremo," One fine day, in Atto Secondo of *Madama Butterfly*. The second act was recorded in the Capital Record Symphony Series and played that spring night on a Silvertone hand crank record player from Sears, Roebuck & Company. The diva Tamaki Miura sang in Italian and her compassionate soprano voice reached into the white pines near the shore of Spirit Lake.

Un bel dì, vedremo
One fine day we will see
Levarsi un fil di fumo sull estremo
A thread of smoke rising
Confin del mare
On the sea in the far horizon
E poi la nave appare
And then the ship appears
Poi la nava bianca

And then the white ship
Entra nel porto
Sails into the harbor
Romba il suo saluto
The thunder of cannons

Hail Mary delivered a melodious soprano wail with slight barks at the start of the aria. Trophy Bay carried out his usual melancholy bay during most of the opera. George Eliot cocked her head with sensational soprano moans near the end of the aria when the diva sang "Entra nel porto" as the ship sails into the harbor. Daniel raised his head, turned to the side, and delivered several hesitant dulcet barks. Dingleberry danced around the wood stove in silence.

benjamin franklin pinkerton
sails back with a greedy american wife
petitions for his son
geisha cio cio san is shamed
stages harakiri with a short sword

Madama Butterfly was a geisha girl who waited three years for the return of Benjamin Franklin Pinkerton, a lieutenant in the United States Navy, but the scoundrel was already married and wanted custody of his son. Cio Cio San was crushed by the deception but consented to the paternal possession and the boy was given an American flag to wave when his father arrived at the house. Madama Butterfly thrust a short sword into her stomach at the end of the opera.

Dummy printed a message on the inside chalk board that "*Madama Butterfly* was only one of more than a hundred opera suicides in the past four centuries. So, how do suicides become fancy operatic performances?"

"Bunker Boy Beaulieu should have staged his suicide as an opera because an abandoned horse stable is not the best story," whispered Poesy May.

"Bunker actually rehearsed more than once the opera of his suicide in a snow bunker," said Big Rant. "Belts around the neck or buckshot in the mouth are not as romantic as snow ghosts and a caved in bunker under the white pine."

"Opera suicides are showy tragedies, imitations of a ghastly death, and never a real escape from the miseries of a reservation," said Bad Boy Aristotle. "Bunker Boy was a shy library cowboy, a solitary outrider, but the crafty snow ghosts were out of season and hardly seductive in a stable."

Bad Boy grieved for the death of Bunker Boy, and at the same time he was inspired by the aria "Un bel dì, verdremo" and moved to tears by the tragic story of Cio Cio San. The next morning, over an everyday bowl of coarse oatmeal and dark maple syrup, Bad Boy created an ironic native opera at the Theatre of Chance.

The *Madama Butterfly* tragic opera was rescripted as the *Ojibwekwe Memengwaa*, or the Ojibwe Butterfly. Ojibwekwe, a comely young native woman, was beguiled by a young courtly Lieutenant in the United States Third Infantry. Thomas Jefferson Dunbar arrived at Leech Lake, Minnesota on October 5, 1898 to subdue native resistance, but the unversed immigrant soldiers under his command were hesitant and outmaneuvered by elusive natives and lost the gratuitous war.

The Ojibwekwe opera was staged two weeks later in the abandoned horse stable near the old Leecy Hotel. The lobby in the stable was simulated with heavy chairs, a broken chest of drawers as a desk, and a wooden ladder was the hotel stairway. The actual horse stables were numbered as hotel rooms and decorated with tattered curtains. Big Rant was perched on a pork barrel in the stable lobby and slowly read out loud the scenes of the opera to a small audience of students and teachers from the government school and natives on the reservation.

Ojibwekwe was visiting relatives nearby when the cocky officer warned her about a risky situation with a cagey native warrior named Hole in the Day. She lowered the umbrella and enlightened the lieutenant that the warrior was her favorite uncle, an honorable native, not a risky adventurer. She started to back away with feigned disdain but could not resist his blue eyes and military gaze, and later they were married in the country way.

The Third Infantry was dispatched the next year to the Philippines, and Dunbar was promoted to captain. Ojibwekwe pretended in a letter that she had given birth to a son and then waited four years for the officer to return to the reservation, but the greedy officer had properly married the barren daughter of a general and insisted on the sole custody of his native son.

Ojibwekwe staged an ironic paternal custody celebration at the Leecy Hotel. Duncey Bass was an orphan, and her native foster mother agreed that the talkative child with the evocative soprano voice of a diva would play a role in the ironic opera *Ojibwekwe Memengwaa*. Duncey was six years old at the time and pretended in the opera to be the daughter of Ojibwekwe.

Poesy May Fairbanks played the assured role of Ojibwekwe. Truman La Chance played the arrogant role of Captain Dunbar, and Dummy Trout carried out the silent and showy gestures of Elizabeth Rose. Master Jean Bonga played a few steady notes on the bugle to honor the presence of an officer.

Brevet Captain Dunbar and his elegant wife Elizabeth Rose arrived at the nearby Ogema Train Station and were ushered by horse carriage to the Leecy Hotel. The captain was in uniform, and the brevet missus wore a white tailored blouse, hobble skirt, and a round straw hat with a huge red bow. The three huge suitcases carried to the stable suite contained either the costumes of gratuitous vanity on a reservation, or the uniforms for an entire platoon of soldiers.

Elizabeth Rose waved to the audience and guests seated in heavy leather chairs. She swished through the lobby and side stepped to the most spacious horse suite in the stable hotel that overlooked the mission pond, telegraph pole, newspaper office, and a native sundries store in the distance.

Elizabeth Rose posed behind the stable bars, removed the straw hat, waggled her long white hair, wiggled her shoulders, pretended to neigh in silence, and then touched a tear on her face with a lacey handkerchief.

The audience burst into laughter, and a stooped boilerman at the government school raised his hand and shouted out his affection for the mute puppeteer, "Dummy, say a word, any word, we want to hear your beautiful voice."

Dummy smiled and pitched the straw hat out of the stable suite. Trophy Boy raised his head and delivered a marvelous bay that echoed in the lobby. Hail Mary simulated a bark and wailed softly. George Eliot faced the old boilerman and moaned. Daniel turned and barked with mercy, and Dingleberry danced around the pork barrel in silence.

The lonesome military wife hunkered down behind the sheer stable curtains, a shadowy figure sidetracked by the heavy scent of straw and wood fires, insistent raven rebukes, the shouts of children near the mission pond, shouts at the telegraph office, and the constant bark of distant mongrels. The opera of tragic custody was an ironic reservation cession of native liberty to the fancy wife of a military officer.

Elizabeth Rose waved once more from behind the sheer curtains, the silhouette of the capricious wife of a military officer in search of a ready family. The capture and adoption of a native child on a treaty reservation was once made easy by the church, state, and military for the poseurs of enlightenment. The curtains moved in the warm summer breeze and the gauzy silhouette of a solitary woman slowly faded away. Dummy created a dream song about the scene in the stable hotel suite. Big Rant turned toward the stable and chanted the dream song.

infantry wives
pose in the wispy light
rehearse the stories of shame
solitary deference
forsaken on a reservation

Bad Boy created three sensational dream song arias for Ojibwekwe. The dream songs were printed in five lines each in the signature style of Dummy Trout. Big Rant sang two of the arias that night in the stable, and the third and last aria was sung by the foster child Duncey Bass. Dummy leaned out of the stable suite, carried out the operatic gestures of hand puppets, and then mouthed the dream songs in silence at the same time.

ojibwekwe is a heart story
consort of pretense
spirit over tradition and temptation
trade beads and leather
dances with an eagle feather

Big Rant delivered the sentiments of a lost romance in the dream song arias with a clear soprano voice. Trophy Bay raised his head and delivered a marvelous melancholy bay. Hail Mary pranced around the pork barrel in the stable and barked left and right with slight hesitations, and the audience applauded the lovely euphony. George Eliot moaned and soughed and raised the straggly white hair on the head of the boilerman. The scene was set for the second dream song aria of the ironic opera.

my child is a girl not your boy
named hole in the day
honored among totemic bears
favors of memory
dream songs in the clouds

Duncey the child entered the opera scene with the name of the warrior Hole in the Day. She wore a black cloche and gray cloak, bright red shoes, and slowly circled the brevet captain.

Elizabeth Rose reached out from the stable suite to touch the native child as her own. Hole in the Day resisted the covetous gestures of the barren military consort, circled the horse stable, and in the company of the magical mongrels sang the aria in a steady soprano voice.

native daughters
stay away from homey hearsay
cozy names and games
soldiers march away to play
chance of memory

Hole in the Day danced around the heavy chairs and pork barrel in the stable and waved at the audience as she slowly sang the last dream song aria and then twice repeated the lines *cozy names and games, soldiers march away to play*. Dummy raised her hands and shouted brava, brava, brava in silence, and the audience was moved to tears by the final aria and the gentle soprano voice of Duncey Bass.

Ojibwekwe waved the golden eagle feather in the last scene of *Ojibwekwe Memengwaa*. Hole in the Day bowed twice, danced in her red shoes around the pork barrel and leather chairs once more, and then ran out of the back of the stable. Captain Dunbar and his brevet missus were shamed by the arias, shamed by their own conceits, and she never understood the tease of an ironic native opera.

Elizabeth Rose was downcast, shamed and desolate with fright that desolate night. She swallowed several poison capsules and was dead by dawn, a showy reservation suicide in the comic tradition of the opéra bouffe.

Dummy stumbled out of the stable suite and collapsed near the pork barrel. She slowly raised her hands to praise the dream song arias in *Ojibwe-kwe Memengwaa*. The audience moved closer to the opera players, and the mongrels moaned, soughed, barked, and with dreamy bays pranced with the stowaways around the stage in the old stable of the Leecy Hotel.

6

POSTCARD HEARSAY

Dummy was roused and ready for the first time in more than fifty years to abandon her silence and shout out loud the names of Wovoka and the Ghost Dance Religion that early morning of a solar eclipse on June 30, 1954 when the sun rose twice over Spirit Lake.

Dummy and the mongrels were out at first light almost every summer morning. The sun moved through the clouds, over the lake and into the white pines as usual, and then slowly a great shadow covered the reservation and the sun rose a second time in less than an hour.

The chickens clucked fitfully, bounced in wild circles, and flapped their wings to escape the gloom, and then rushed back to the shed and under the cabins. Songbirds were silenced by the great shadow, and the curious, hesitant croak and tender caw of distant ravens was an ominous sound. The loyal mongrels were silent at first, and then moaned and bayed in singular harmony with the second rise of the sun that morning.

Dummy Trout sauntered more than a mile to the post office once a week with the five mongrels to collect the mail, no matter the season or the weather, but she has not received an actual letter or postcard since the end of the Second World War.

She visited the post office several times a week in the past, and gathered with other natives at The Pioneer Store, Chippewa Bank, telegraph office, and gestured in silence to guests at three hotels on the reservation, the Hiawatha, the Headquarters, and the more pleasurable Leecy Hotel with a great dining room, once a week opera broadcasts on a large radio console, and a charming horse carriage service from the Ogema Train Station.

Augustus Hudon Beaulieu published two newspapers more than thirty years ago on the reservation, *The Progress* and later *The Tomahawk*. The weekly editorials were keen and critical of federal policies, and readers were up to date on international and local news, native hearsay, and national product advertisements, but the sources of news slowly changed with the

entire country after the First World War. Natives were drafted and enlisted
to serve in the military, automobiles slowly replaced horses, and national
news was broadcast regularly on cheap mail order radios from Sears, Roebuck & Company.

The Tomahawk ended soon after the death of the publisher, and then
the bank, two of the three hotels, the one night a week movie theatre,
and many other reservation businesses closed, and only the post office remained after two world wars. Many native families moved to cities for education and job training after the wars, and the once lively native culture
of the reservation was reduced to fur trade lore and legends, nostalgia for
the shamans and tent shakers, treaty hearsay, suicide counts, forecasts of
resentments, envies and vengeance, and stories of the desperate course of
the Great Depression.

Basile Hudon Beaulieu wrote fifty letters or chronicles to the mute puppeteer and the heirs of the fur trade over thirteen years starting on October
2, 1932. The fifty chronicles were about the rise of fascist factions, protests
of labor unions, socialist coalitions, and the lively encounters of his artistic
brother Aloysius with *impressionnisme*, avant-garde artistic creations, sur-
realism, and the deceptive rush of social realism in literature a few years
before the Nazi Occupation of France. The chronicles were printed on the
old newspaper press and given away on the reservation.

Dummy once counted the days to the next chronicle with stories about
native relations and the dauntless puppet parleys that teased the fascists
and mocked Adolf Hitler and the wicked march of the Third Reich. She
likened the tease, resistance, and native mockery of fascist federal agents on
treaty reservations to the courageous movements of the French Résistance.

The final chronicle about Romain Roland, the novelist and historian,
was posted on January 3, 1945. The French literary artist created the critical
concept of *littérature engagée*, the ethos and constancy of literary engage-
ment. Dummy associated the good fight for French literature and liberty to
the great spirit of native dream songs, mockery of the devious government,
and the natural tease of trickster stories as cultural resistance.

The Theatre of Chance hand puppet parleys were dramatic and ironic
encounters with snow ghosts and federal agents and the chase of churchy
hope and state treachery over resources on the reservation. The puppet

parleys, heart stories, and dreams songs were a native ethos and resistance to federal policies at the same time. Dummy printed a new dream song on the inside chalk board about the literary ethos of silence and resistance.

churchy marionettes
double agents of the federal reich
cruise with timber barons
count of timber stumps
revealed in native mockery

The saunter through the white pine and birch and around the mission pond was more social than postal. Dummy was always amused when the clerk at the post office, a native woman who retired as an assistant school librarian and returned to sort the mail on the reservation, enhanced postcard messages with quirky hearsay.

Postcard Mary was short, sturdy, buoyant, and teased with many nicknames in the past sixty years, Deck Hand, Post Hound, Roman Thumb, Sticky Lips, Dinky Paws, Sorry Stamp, and more, but the critical comparison to Typhoid Mary was cruel because the crazy stories that Postcard Mary concocted from ordinary postcards were ironic and never vindictive, crude, or deadly. The hearsay versions of the postcards that she created were always more memorable than the originals, and that was the marvelous creative tease of Postcard Mary.

Dummy was silent, of course, and earned the respect of the postal clerk who treated the mongrels one by one with tiny bites of pemmican, and at the same time, she related strange hearsay and heart stories based on recent postcards.

Natives quibbled about the cock and bull scenes, but hardly anyone resisted the obvious, the enhanced postcard stories had become the mainstay of native communal hearsay even though the actual content was scarcely recognizable after the catchy stories created by Postcard Mary. The postcard addressed to the mission priest last week, for instance, noted that a distant relative had given birth to twins, "Two lovely flights of creation landed with the sacred favors of our Savior."

Postcard Mary always turned to the window and the trees when she started a postcard story, and some natives speculated that the hearsay was created by either a gifted storier or tricksters in the clouds. "The mission priest was recently visited twice by Jesus Christ, who flew a great distance in a sacred seaplane and landed with the favor of natives on the Mission Pond" was the hearsay version by Postcard Mary.

Dummy printed a note in response, "Overnight flights and resurrections on the reservation, and you were the first to see the avian light of native Jesus." Trophy Bay presented a mellow moan as she printed the note, and two other postal mongrels carried on with gentle barks and moans. Big John, a mongrel foxhound, smiled, sighed, and wagged his tail. Tallulah, a bold beagle and husky, raised her head, cocked her ears, and then joined the other mongrel moans with a heavenly contralto bay.

Dummy received a creased postcard a week later from Paris, France with a faint picture of the Eiffel Tower. By Now Rose Beaulieu, who served as a hospital nurse with *La Résistance* in Paris, wrote in a tiny and perfect government school script, "We arrive in a few weeks by ship, train, and bus, Basile, Aloysius, and my giant lover Prometheus. Depart tomorrow on the Île de France for New York, so sort out the hand puppets and cue the mongrels for new opera stories and an autumn parley. Need two cabins near the Theatre of Chance."

Postcard Mary created an extraordinary story based on the postcard and a few days later the hearsay had circulated on the reservation. "Basile Hudon Beaulieu and his brother Aloysius were partisans in *La Résistance* and captured during the Nazis Occupation of Paris, and at the end of the war the native author and artist were honored at the Eiffel Tower by General Charles de Gaulle and then sent back on the Île de France to create a new fur trade ethos of culture and democracy with the fire sticks stolen by the giant trickster named Prometheus."

Basile, Aloysius, By Now, and Prometheus boarded the restored Île de France at Le Havre on Tuesday, August 30, 1955 and arrived a week later at Pier 88 in New York. The opulence of the celebrated ocean liner had been disguised in gray paint to serve as an allied troop ship and evade enemy submarines during the Second World War in the North Atlantic.

Basile and Aloysius, native veterans of the First World War, had sailed on the Île de France to Le Havre on July 30, 1932 in a bargain cabin during the Great Depression. They mocked the casual patricians and stagy pretenders on board that summer with stories about native shamans and teased the deck readers that Jay Gatsby in *The Great Gatsby* by F. Scott Fitzgerald was outwitted by seductive native snow ghosts on the White Earth Reservation.

Thousands of rich and footloose passengers sailed in cabins of splendor over the affluent years, and then at the end of the Second World War, combat soldiers waited on the gray deck with anticipation as the magical ship entered the Hudson River and slowly moved toward the terminal of liberty in the United States.

Basile and Aloysius returned after more than twenty years and revealed their nostalgia for the Museum of Modern Art and the singular scent of old books at Biblo and Tannen Bookstore on the corner of Ninth Street and Fourth Avenue in New York City. They walked with By Now and Prometheus down Tenth Avenue that balmy afternoon to Greenwich Village, and rented two rooms at the Hotel Earle at Washington Square. They were told several times that Ernest Hemingway and Dylan Thomas once stayed at the same hotel.

Charles de Gaulle resigned as the provisional president on January 20, 1946, and nine months later voters supported the Constitution of the French Fourth Republic. Basile and Aloysius were ready to leave the country when De Gaulle was not elected as president, and three years later they were even more convinced to escape when the fascist collaborator René Bousquet received a suspended sentence for his untold crimes against humanity and for the execution of Operation Spring Breeze, the removal of the Jews of Paris to the *Vélodrome d'Hiver* and then to the internment camp at Drancy in early July 1942.

Nathan Crémieux persuaded Basile, Aloysius, By Now, and Prometheus to remain and work with *La Résistance* to expose the poseurs who had collaborated with the Nazi Occupation and Vichy Regime. They stayed and were active for nine more years but would never respect the 1953 Bordeaux court trial of enemy soldiers who carried out the massacre of the good citizens in Oradour sur Glane on June 10, 1944, four days after the allied landing at Normandy.

Nathan Crémieux invited artists, authors, gallery owners, and members of *La Résistance* to celebrate the marriage of By Now Rose Beaulieu to the rangy raconteur Prometheus Postma on Saturday, August 13, 1955, at the Galerie Ghost Dance in Paris. By Now surprised everyone because she had vowed every other day never to marry, but her cousins Basile and Aloysius were never convinced.

Her first great lover was William Huska, a migrant butcher from Lithuania and veteran of the First World War who was shot in the heart more than twenty years ago by the police at a national protest of the Bonus Expeditionary Force near the Capitol in Washington.

Prometheus, a raconteur with a magical smile, was waiting early one morning under a lamppost on Rue de la République in Bandol, France. He wore huge raffia espadrilles, purple trousers, white gloves, a long gray overcoat, and carried a metal suitcase with *Célébrité de Rien*, Celebrity of Nothing, painted on one side, and *Le Raconteur de la Liberté* on the other side. He was waiting for a chance ride to Marseille and then for the double chance to obtain a visa to California.

Prometheus told stories about the Yahi native named Ishi who was rescued in northern California more than thirty years earlier by the anthropologist Alfred Kroeber. The Frisian was inspired by Ishi and ready to live with natives in the mountains of Northern California. By Now resisted the raconteur at first, but a few months later she was overcome with his marvelous heart stories, true gestures, and the enormous gentle hands of the giant Frisian. Prometheus was stateless, an outsider with no passport, visa, or state documents.

Nathan had provided a counterfeit passport of the United States of America, but that was only a desperate measure during the Nazi Occupation of Paris. A marriage certificate could more easily secure a visa, but first it was necessary to become a citizen of France. Nathan easily documented the honorable service of the raconteur as an active member of *La Résistance* in Paris and later at Sanary-sur-Mer on the Mediterranean Sea.

7

HEART STORIES

Dummy Trout carved three puppet heads, and as the facial features slowly emerged from the blocks of fallen birch trees, she became more elusive about one of the new hand puppets. Once the puppet heads were preened, the arms and hands connected and toned, and the bodies clothed, she smiled and revealed the original postcard from By Now Rose Beaulieu.

The Baron of Patronia, the extraordinary native healer who created panic holes on the meadow, was one of the new puppets. The second puppet was a remarkable resemblance of By Now, and the puppet seemed to hold back for more time to be carved. The bold features were reminiscent of the story of her birth and given name.

By Now was born more than a month late and on every overdue day her father bragged that she had waited long enough to learn a few languages. "That child should've been here by now," her father shouted to the trickster of nativity, and a baby girl finally arrived on a warm spring morning. The jovial public health doctor entered By Now on the official birth certificate as her given name.

Dummy printed a concise command on the inside chalk board, "Bad Boy Aristotle must carve the head of the puppet Prometheus." Naturally he was the only stowaway who could sculpt from imagination the faces of classical figures because he had created lively native scenes and characters so deftly from the burned pages of *Poetics* by Aristotle.

Bad Boy considered the gods, poets, healers, and the great demons in ancient stories when he carved from birch the head of Prometheus and related the elusive native trickster to the deities of classical literature. The cultural hero was sculpted with heavy eyebrows, angular chin, strong jowls, a broad brow, and gentle, seductive eyes that were tinted blue. Bad Boy recited a dream song a few days later and presented the stately hand puppet named Prometheus.

bad boy prometheus
mocked the fascists of misery
courted by now and liberty
celebrities of resistance
theatre of chance puppet shows

Dummy imagined her lover Nookaa who died more than fifty years ago in a forest fire as the glorious puppet Prometheus. Bunker Boy would have considered the hand puppet an outrider cowboy and stayed for the parley of liberty. La Chance pointed out the stalwart features of the puppet as his heroic father the soldier of memory. Big Rant envisioned an obscure father in the stature of Prometheus. Poesy May created a romantic poem about the new classical hand puppet. Bad Boy pictured a stately hand puppet that inspired relations, dream songs, and trickster stories of native liberty at the Theatre of Chance.

Dummy finally revealed the secret hand puppet as the carved visage of herself with a wide smile, rounded cheeks, and a great polished dome decorated with long straggly white hair. She pointed to her head as the actual source of the hair on the puppet. Dummy the hand puppet was ready for the first time to take part in the parley, and the voice of the silent puppet was presented by Big Rant.

Bad Boy Aristotle lived up to his native name and secretly created one more hand puppet with remnants found in a trash heap, a puppet close to the hideous demon he once constructed from an ordinary tin of Maxwell House Coffee. He had already carved a birch puppet head of Prometheus, and the secret puppet was a creative portrayal of the Trickster of Liberty fashioned from a tin cone of Red Wing Premium Beer. Two great red wings decorated the cone and framed a romantic image of a native figure with a full headdress. Bad Boy painted with red lipstick the word Trickster between the words "Premium" and "Beer" and dressed the trickster in a black tuxedo with a crisp white collar. The blunt yellow fingers of the beer cone trickster were pencil stubs.

The new puppets were groomed and ready for the grand return of the native troupe after more than twenty years in Paris, France. John Clement Beaulieu, a combat engineer in the First World War, waited overnight for his relatives Basile, Aloysius, By Now, and the venerable newcomer Prometheus at the train station in Detroit Lakes and delivered the envoys of resistance and liberty to the Theatre of Chance.

Basile and Aloysius moved into a familiar cabin that was once located near Misaabe and his four perceptive mongrels, Mona Lisa, Ghost Moth, Nosey, and Shimmer, on the wooded shoreline of Bad Boy Lake about two miles from the Theatre of Chance at Spirit Lake.

Misaabe, an elusive native healer, lived in a cabin nearby more than thirty years ago when Basile struggled to overcome the nightmares of combat, the recurring dreams of mangled soldiers and horses, combined chunks of brain and bone, and hordes of flies on the bloody mush of bodies in the First World War. Basile told the healer that he could not escape the hideous sounds and ghastly scenes of war, and every insect in flight at night became the sound of the enemy. The mighty healer listened and then related heart stories about an opera of blue flies that bounced on a lantern and droned around the cabin. The main blue fly landed in a spider web and could not escape, and the other flies circled the web to distract the spider.

Misaabe carried on with the evasive fly stories night after night, a continuous ironic tease of an everlasting opera of blue flies. Basile was distracted by the changeable stories and finally learned the obvious from the old healer that heart stories were trickster scenes created from one story to another. The reveals of native heart stories were chancy flights of natural motion that countered customs, recitations, and a single recount of memory.

Basile was almost healed when he created stories about the nightmares, the ironic variations of fate and fright. The maggots on bloody soldiers turned into flies and naturally flew away in the mutable scenes of a gruesome opera. He learned to tease dreary situations of misery with heart stories, renounce the old torments of sincerity and sympathy, overturn repetitions and the scary exhibitions of memory, reverse heavy traditions with mockery, and salute the maggots that were liberated on the bloody soldiers as glorious flies of memory in the nightmare operas of the First World War.

Basile created dream songs and stories of natural motion, and his brother perceived the natural blue hues and shimmer of ravens. Aloysius never painted black ravens despite the godly rave of the mission priest who favored unnatural and demonic black, black, black. The Great War incited mockery of dangerous and clumsy commanders, but he painted some miniature scenes in combat, and later he created spectacular abstract scenes of blue ravens at the Café du Dome in Paris. Pablo Picasso was pictured as a blue raven with a huge cubist beak. Guillaume Apollinaire was portrayed as a giant melancholy raven on the Pont Mirabeau over the River Seine.

Aloysius was a visionary painter of natural motion, abstract waves of color, contours, and shadows, and was inspired by the original native images on stone, hide, bark, and the untutored native ledger artists who were held as political prisoners at Fort Marion in Saint Augustine, Florida. Later he was inspired by the ethereal blues in the magical scenes painted by Marc Chagall.

Aloysius was thirteen years old when he first painted blue ravens, abstract ravens in natural motion on flimsy newsprint provided by *The Tomahawk*, an independent newspaper published by his uncle Augustus Hudon Beaulieu. Aloysius and Basile were hired by their uncle to hawk the weekly newspaper at the Ogema Train Station.

Aloysius never thought about painting the blue flies on the dead bodies of combat soldiers and only envisioned blue ravens in the birch trees, cemetery monuments, and telegraph wires on the reservation. Mostly he mourned the absence of any birds on the decimated battlefields of France. Months later at the end of the war he painted abstract blue raven scenes at famous bridges over the River Seine. In one painting he created stone bastions near the Pont Neuf with great abstract ravens on enormous crests of white and blue river waves. Aloysius revealed at the gallery exhibition that he was inspired by *The Great Wave*, the famous woodblock by Katsushika Hokusai. Nathan scheduled an exhibition of his most recent paintings, *Trente Six Scènes des Corbeaux Bleus*, Thirty-Six Scenes of Blue Ravens, at the Galerie Crémieux in Paris.

Aloysius continued to paint en plein air during the Nazi Occupation of France. His abstract ravens soared in visionary scenes with the minimal wash of blue wings and traces of rouge in a new style of totemic fauvism. Nathan named him the native resistance envoy of blue totemic ravens in the monstrous world of nationalists, deadly collaborators, and devious cringers of the Vichy Regime.

The generous sense of natural motion in his abstract blue ravens changed to fractured images of totemic animals and birds four years later at the end of the Nazi Occupation of Paris. The strange ruptured bones, claws, paws, twisted wing feathers, contorted motion of ravens, fractured and cubist faces of beaver, bear, marten, wolf, fox, river otter, golden eagle, and many other totemic animals and birds of the fur trade were created for the exhibition *Totemic Custody and Casualty*, along with the solemn display of Ghost Dance shirts at the new *Galerie de la Danse des Esprits*, Galerie Ghost Dance, established at the end of the war by Nathan Crémieux.

Aloysius returned to the reservation, and once again, he was obsessed with the sway of trees and shimmer of colors on Bad Boy Lake. For more than a month he waited in silence on the shoreline to observe the slightest breeze over the lake, the creases and eddies of natural motion, and the traces and abstract hues of the seasons. He created more than thirty new abstract scenes of the lake in natural motion, the wild colors of totemic chance. The new watercolor scenes were much larger than his previous paintings.

Dummy wrote on the inside chalk board, "Aloysius has created that totemic chance of a blue dance of natural motion in the eyes of honeybees and hummingbirds."

By Now Beaulieu and Prometheus occupied a cozy cabin nearby on the shoreline of Bad Boy Lake. They heard the slow sound of waves at night, the laughter and plaintive sing out of loons, and the steady thump, thump, thump of moths on the window. The dilapidated cabin was a native sanctuary for the two resistance warriors with their memories of the occupation and an escape distance from enemy soldiers at every corner of memory. The morning light bounced in the white pine, maple, and birch, and the shadows wavered in the cabin as the natural motion of liberty.

The new hand puppets were polished and decked out with coats and capes a few days later and prepared for the overnight summer parley around a bonfire. The four stowaways created and rehearsed the colloquies for the puppets, and the mongrels were at the ready to moan, groan, bark, yodel, bay, and bounce with every gesture of the hand puppets.

The fire circle parley was carried out once or twice every summer on a spectacular meadow of panic holes created by the Baron of Patronia, the dauntless native who counted with giant steps a federal land grant in his name and declared the natural meadow of panic holes and curative shouts the outright sway of chance and native liberty.

The Baron of Patronia has buried his solemn shouts in seven panic holes for more than thirty years, one for each distinct pose, mood, manner, temper, and fury of resistance to cultural fakery, promissory missions, outright misery, and the predatory state of greedy governance on a federal treaty reservation.

He shouted into the first panic hole to bury the steady rage over the mercenary fur trade and ruins of totemic solidarity. His temper and shouts over the poseurs of native traditions and the carousel of feigned political creation stories were buried in the second panic hole. In the third panic hole he buried the eternal anger over the plunder of white pine by federal agents and timber barons. He buried great shouts of sorrow over native suicides in the fourth panic hole. His wrath over native want and starvation on the reservation was shouted year after year into the fifth panic hole. He shouted in the sixth panic hole over the absence of mockery and irony in new native stories. The seventh panic hole was reserved for his great fury and resistance to the seductive snow ghosts.

Dummy teased the Baron of Patronia in a song poem and passed the chalk board around the bonfire. Big Rant leaned closer to the fire and read the concise poem out loud.

baron of patronia
shouts out and never pouts
favors panic holes
great meadows of native liberty
buries missions of misery

Native shouts and panic holes were necessary to heal the heart, and the shouters became stronger storiers in the sway of liberty. Bad Boy shouted into panic holes to heal his anger and shame, and then turned his shouts into creative stories of burned books. Poesy May once circled the old panic holes and heard the eerie native echoes of betrayal, of cultural humiliation, and fury, but the distant wavers of shouts were clumsy, seldom poetic, and since then she has only returned to the meadow of panic for the summer hand puppet parleys.

Master Jean should have shouted out his rage into a panic hole when his mother was diagnosed with tuberculosis and sent to the Ahgwahching

State Sanatorium. Bunker Boy might have mocked the scriptures of hope, shame, separation, and shouted into more than one panic hole, and outlived the cowboys and snow ghosts to create his own outrider puppet parleys at the Theatre of Chance.

Dummy raised Prometheus on her right hand and Dummy the puppet on her left hand. The great fire created shadows that danced on the polished faces of the puppets. Prometheus turned his head from side to side and gestured to everyone in the circle. The hand puppet leaned down and pretended to shout into a panic hole near the circle of fire. Trophy Boy moved closer to the circle, raised his head, and almost shouted his bay. Dingleberry danced around the fire and yodeled. George Eliot turned her head to the side and moaned with the mercy of a great soprano diva. Dummy the healer was heard once more in the bold voice of Big Rant. Bad Boy was the modest voice of the gentle hand puppet Prometheus.

> DUMMY: Greek gods must have concocted nicknames.
> PROMETHEUS: By Now is one of the great nicknames.
> DUMMY: She created many nicknames and heart stories.
> PROMETHEUS: Greek gods were never my natives.
> DUMMY: Almost Native and Just About are nicknames.
> PROMETHEUS: Celebrity of Nothing was my name.
> DUMMY: Nothing is a tease and an ironic nickname.
> PROMETHEUS: By Now named me About Time.
> DUMMY: Yes, about time she found you a nickname.
> PROMETHEUS: About Time and Celebrity of Nothing.
> DUMMY: By Now teases everyone with a nickname.
> PROMETHEUS: Heart storiers always create the way.
> DUMMY: By Now rode Treaty to Capitol Hill.
> PROMETHEUS: Rightly honored in two world wars.
> DUMMY: By Now was born a maestro of mockery.
> PROMETHEUS: My father was an artist of mockery.
> DUMMY: Mockery is the chancy art of resistance.
> PROMETHEUS: Count on me as a chancy raconteur.
> DUMMY: The Theatre of Chance is our native liberty.
> PROMETHEUS: By Now was my chance of liberty.
> DUMMY: Native chance is our sense of presence.

PROMETHEUS: *Le Corbeau Bleu* to Sanary-sur-Mer.

DUMMY: Place de Grève to Oradour-sur-Glane.

PROMETHEUS: By Now liberated soldiers with teases.

DUMMY: Another tricky catch at the Theatre of Chance.

PROMETHEUS: Resistance is our chancy liberty.

Basile Hudon Beaulieu was almost shied when Dummy presented a bundle of fifty letters that he wrote to the heirs of the fur trade over thirteen years. The yellowy newsprint letters were printed on the old rotary press of *The Progress* and *The Tomahawk* and given away at the post office, government school, Ogema Train Station, and at the Leecy Hotel.

Big Rant slowly read out loud from the letter "Celebrity of Nothing" dated November 2, 1940. "Prometheus was actually a raconteur of futurity and celebrity of nothing, as his stories of exile created a sense of motion rather than destiny. He assumed from the name on the side of the van, our faces, and gestures, that we were natives, and with that assurance he slowly climbed into the back of the van, and at once related an elusive story about a native named Ishi."

Prometheus waited that early morning near the corner of Rue de la République in Bandol on the Côte d'Azur for a chance ride to Marseille when native puppeteers in a large van named *Les Marionnettes Bleues* pulled over near the lamppost to admire the spectacular height of the raconteur, more than seven feet high, who wore bizarre clown clothes. He was an *apatride* or stateless raconteur from East Frisia in the Netherlands on his chancy way to California.

Prometheus was nosed by the mongrels, and when the wild operatic moans and bays slowly ended, everyone gathered around the fire circle and celebrated the raconteur as a favored stowaway at the Theatre of Chance.

Irene Martin Vizenor, manager at the Ponsford Post Office and former reservation schoolteacher, was at the puppet parley. She was an advocate of education and the trust of native stories as the source of irony and native wisdom. Postcard Mary and many other natives were at the parley, including the librarian Harmony Baswewe, Carmen Bear with an outlier surveyor at hand for the night, several teachers, students, and three curious anthropology graduate students from the University of Minnesota.

Dummy circled the fire and raised By Now on her right hand and the

Baron of Patronia on her left hand. The mongrels were at her side, and the fire flashed in their eyes. Big Rant was the bold voice of By Now. Master Jean delivered the rush and dramatic shouts of the Baron of Patronia.

BY NOW: Native rage is buried in panic holes.

BARON: Creation stories are shouts, never whispers.

BY NOW: Shout out the great names in native history.

BARON: Hole in the Day shouted in many panic holes.

BY NOW: Shamans shout tricky cures to the clouds.

BARON: Shouts last and dream songs float away.

BY NOW: Snow ghosts are chased away in panic holes.

BARON: Thousands since the horror of the fur trade.

BY NOW: Millions of native shouts buried in the earth.

BARON: Flowers bloom on the meadow of panic holes.

BY NOW: Some natives shout at the fish in ice holes.

BARON: Frozen shouts melt away with the season.

BY NOW: Every native must shout into a panic hole.

BARON: Everywhere the earth waits for our shouts.

BY NOW: Natives in the city shout under bridges.

BARON: Panic holes are in parks and church yards.

BY NOW: No panic holes on the fur trade routes.

BARON: Totemic animals shouted into panic holes.

BY NOW: Shamans and wolves shout at full moons.

BARON: Shouts about the snow ghosts of suicide.

BY NOW: Bunker never shouted into a panic hole.

BARON: Seduced by shame and the snow ghosts.

BY NOW: Dummy shouts in silence on the page.

BARON: Silent shouts are heard in heart stories.

BY NOW: Dream songs are her silent shouts.

BARON: Some heart stories are silent panic holes.

BY NOW: Ready to shout into a panic hole of fire.

BARON: The rage of liberty is a panic hole of fire.

BY NOW: Native shouts of resistance and liberty.

The Baron of Patronia and the stowaways shouted into the fire and the mongrels barked and bayed at the end of the puppet parley. George Eliot raised the timbre of the mongrel moans with a singular soprano bay. Tallulah the beagle mongrel delivered a harmonic contralto bay. Daniel united with the bays and then turned away.

By Now, Basile, and Aloysius shouted their praise for the great puppets and the marvelous parley as Prometheus slowly moved closer to the circle of fire. He wore white gloves and mimed an applause in silence. Trophy Bay followed the giant mime around the fire with a melancholy baritone bay.

Harmony Baswewe celebrated the dedication and silent genius of Dummy Trout and the five stowaways for the great performances, but the praise was interrupted because the parley was not yet over. Bad Boy shouted out that there was one last hand puppet parley. Prometheus and the mongrels circled the fire for a surprise parley with the hand puppet Prometheus and a crudely decorated tin cone of Red Wing Premium Beer as the hand puppet named the Trickster of Liberty.

La Chance was the lively voice of the Trickster of Liberty and Bad Boy was the voice of the puppet Prometheus. Together they created and rehearsed the esoteric back talk of the pirate of fire and the native trickster with classical sources from burned books recovered by Bad Boy.

By Now smiled and Dummy raised her hands in silent praise of the puppet parley. Trophy Bay moved closer to the two stowaways and softly moaned. Tallulah sneezed with favor, and then bayed. Dingleberry yodeled around the fire and the other chorus mongrels raised their heads ready to moan, bounce, and bark with the performance.

> TRICKSTER: You were exiled from an elite democracy.
> PROMETHEUS: Yes, more godly temper than ironic play.
> TRICKSTER: Treaties were not the work of a Darian League.
> PROMETHEUS: Gods favor power, feign hope for humanity.
> TRICKSTER: The enemies of chance are hope and pity.
> PROMETHEUS: Mockery was my course not stolen fire.
> TRICKSTER: Listen to the mongrel as a chorus of chance.
> PROMETHEUS: The heroic gods devised a deadly fate.
> TRICKSTER: Tricksters steal fire and create ironic stories.
> PROMETHEUS: Miserly gods owned fire and lightning.
> TRICKSTER: Not the silence between lightning and thunder.
> PROMETHEUS: Silence is a chorus of peace and liberty.

TRICKSTER: Godly betrayal and torment in your name.

PROMETHEUS: Only to the pompous gods of obedience.

TRICKSTER: Trickster stories outwit the tyranny of gods.

PROMETHEUS: Poseurs of craft are weaker than necessity.

TRICKSTER: Creation stories are ironies of necessity.

PROMETHEUS: Fascists never escape the furies of fate.

TRICKSTER: The Theatre of Chance counters destiny.

PROMETHEUS: Frisian raconteurs mock the myths of fate.

TRICKSTER: The tricksters tease and imitate noble actions.

PROMETHEUS: Tragedy is the imitation of pitiable action.

TRICKSTER: Shamans play out the poses of insecure people.

PROMETHEUS: Aeschylus revealed the deceit of courage.

TRICKSTER: Chance overturns dominance and shame.

PROMETHEUS: Yes, the gods create a most anxious sight.

TRICKSTER: Do not hide from what must be endured.

PROMETHEUS: Natives dare to care and with no shame.

TRICKSTER: Monotheism undermined totemic stories.

PROMETHEUS: The theft of fire teases the future of death.

TRICKSTER: Dream songs are in the clouds not graves.

PROMETHEUS: Heroic myths of me planted blind hope.

TRICKSTER: Promises are the feigned cultures of nothing.

PROMETHEUS: The myth of my name was never me.

TRICKSTER: The tease of my name must last forever.

Poesy May moved closer to the fire circle and surprised the troupe with a dramatic reading of a short selection from the first act of *Prometheus Unbound* by Percy Bysshe Shelley. Dummy and the native troupe were delighted because Poesy May was a native whisperer when she arrived as a runaway. She was almost silent at first and then one clear night she pointed to the sky and boldly named the great constellations, Orion, Ursa Major, Gemini, and The Pleiades. Later she created native names for the same three constellations, *Waawaatesi*, or Firefly for Orion, *Nimishoomis*, or Grandfather for Ursa Major, and *Nimisenyag*, or Sisters for The Pleiades.

Poesy May chanted, "the stars move forever and stay, never fade away," and later she announced the names of great natives, "Hole in the Day, Sitting Bull, Chief Joseph, and Standing Bear, who stay and display as great constellations a sense of natural motion, presence, and liberty."

She turned away shame, malicious threats, and teases with creative names of the constellation, and she learned to deftly whisper down the churchy curses and wordy abuse of chance with the names of native leaders. Trophy Bay waited in silence for the sound of her gentle voice.

> No change, no pause, no hope! Yet, I endure.
> I ask the Earth, have not the mountains felt?
> I ask the Heaven, the all-beholding sun,
> Has it not seen? The Sea, in storm or calm,
> Heaven's ever-changing shadow, spread below,
> Have its deaf waves not heard my agony?
> Ah me! Alas, pain, pain ever, forever!

Dummy served native corn soup, warm beer, and blueberry mush on crackers to celebrate the poetry and puppet parleys of the native troupe and stowaways that night at the Theatre of Chance. By Now raised each of the hand puppets and mocked the deceptive promises of an elite democracy, "show me the course of liberty not separatism," and "hand puppets, panic holes, and corn soup are the stays of heart stories and native liberty." Prometheus raised his hands to the open joists of the cabin and simulated a slow swing to the table of food.

Poesy May created two new phrases of the poem by Percy Bysshe Shelley, "have the federal agents not heard the agony, the native pain, the eternal misery of separation on reservations."

Big Rant selected the second to the last letter written from Paris by Basile Beaulieu, Wednesday, October 25, 1944, and read out loud late that night creative versions of the first two original paragraphs from the yellowy newspaper print.

"The heirs of the fur trade endure with shame and remorse of the colonial wars over beaver, marten, and mink. New France voyageurs and native perpetrators of peltry are romanced in literature, and natives have waited centuries to hear the legion of honors for the sacrifice of totemic animals, or at least to witness the sway of human and animal rights, but peace and liberty are only sentiments declared in constitutional democracies.

"New France secured a union of natives in the great cause and commerce of peltry, and missions of peace and continental liberty, but no colonial treaty could ever restore the natural motion of totemic associations with animals and birds that natives and our relations culled and ravaged in the centuries of the fur trade."

The Theatre of Chance mongrels, Trophy Bay, Hail Mary, George Eliot, Daniel, and Dingleberry, and the two post office mongrels, Tallulah and Big John, became a chorus of sighs, bays, marvelous moans, and mellow barks to celebrate the poetry and puppet parleys and to honor the memory of distant relations and the totemic animals that were massacred in the fur trade.

8

WHITEY DWIGHTY

The Theatre of Chance was connected to electricity a few years ago so Dummy could hear the mellow commentaries of Milton Cross and radio broadcasts of the Metropolitan Opera. Last week she listened to the performance of *Don Giovanni* by Wolfgang Amadeus Mozart, and once more the mongrels were roused by the overture and raised their heads to moan, sough, and bay in marvelous harmony.

Dummy heard the first network broadcast of the opera *Hänsel und Gretel* more than twenty years ago and other live opera broadcasts on the huge console radio at the Leecy Hotel every Saturday. Native stories, postcard hearsay, train station gossip, and the lively backchat of guests once a week at the hotel were continued with the troupe of stowaways, mongrels, and other relations at live radio broadcasts at the Theatre of Chance.

Dummy summoned the native troupe of stowaways to gather around the Silvertone radio purchased from Sears, Roebuck & Company to hear the live broadcast of the inaugural address of President John F. Kennedy and a singsong reading of "The Gift Outright" by the celebrated poet Robert Frost. Trophy Bay was always ready to bay but the other mongrels waited for the opera music and simply groaned over the steady pitch and mood of political speeches on the radio.

"President Eisenhower, Vice President Nixon, President Truman, fellow citizens, we observe today not a victory of party, but a celebration of freedom," declared President Kennedy.

"The world is very different now. For man holds in his mortal hands the power to abolish all forms of human poverty and all forms of human life.

"And so, my fellow Americans: ask not what your country can do for you, ask what you can do for your country."

President Kennedy served in combat and was a decorated veteran, and the strong, generous tone of his voice awakened the nation to a renewed spirit of governance. The decorous mention of Dwight Eisenhower at the inauguration, however, reminded Basile, By Now, and Aloysius of the protest march that summer almost thirty years earlier with the Bonus Expeditionary Force.

The Bonus Army was a stouthearted muster of more than twenty thousand veterans of the First World War. The veterans camped on the National Mall, at Anacostia Flats, and in vacant buildings in Washington. Basile, Aloysius, and By Now were there with other native veterans from other treaty reservations around the country to demand the government provide war veterans with more than a Tombstone Bonus.

By Now has told many stories about how she cantered on a horse named Treaty across six states to march with veterans but seldom mentioned that she camped with a lover named William Hushka near the National Mall. The cash bonus was approved in the House of Representatives but vetoed by the Senate. President Herbert Hoover ordered the immediate eviction of the veterans from Washington. The edgy police advanced to remove the honorable veterans, and during the resistance and violent commotion, Hushka was shot in the heart. Other veterans and their families were rousted from the city by soldiers with bayonets under the command of General Douglas MacArthur, army chief of staff, and his obedient aide Major Dwight Eisenhower. By Now returned to the reservation with her loyal horse Treaty after the military services held for her lover at Arlington National Cemetery.

Basile and Aloysius were betrayed once again by the federal government, and by military commanders, first as natives who were not counted as citizens of the country at the time, and then as veterans who were promised a bonus for honorable combat service in the First World War. They decisively abandoned the bonus claims, mocked the deceptive politicians, and decided to visit Hard Luck Town and other lively encampments of war veterans along the East River in New York City. They toured the Hoovervilles, browsed at the Biblo and Tannen Booksellers, city missions, and the Metropolitan Museum of Art. Basile and Aloysius boarded the Île de France a few weeks later and gladly returned to the great galleries and sense of liberty in Paris.

Dummy has never traveled outside the treaty boundaries of the reservation since the Great Hinckley Fire. Yet she envisioned many spirited scenes in the fifty letters to the heirs of the fur trade written by Basile. She could easily outline the episodes in every letter and that morning pointed to the chapter "Solemn Repose, August 27, 1944."

Big Rant read out loud a section about General Eisenhower, or Whitey Dwighty, a nickname he earned during the liberation of Paris. "General Charles de Gaulle was resolute that the Free French Forces would lead the liberation celebration and parade down the Champs-Élysées to the Place de la Concorde. The Supreme Allied Commander General Dwight Eisenhower had another master plan. Whitey Dwighty agreed that the French soldiers could lead the liberation march, but only if the soldiers were white, not black.

"General Eisenhower turned back the black soldiers, the most loyal and valorous in military service, and denied black colonial soldiers the right to be seen in the liberation parade. Georges Dukson, a wounded black warrior of *La Résistance* in Paris, was scorned and pushed aside by military officers during the liberation parade.

"How could any officer disrespect the Tirailleurs Sénégalais who served with courage in the infantry, fought against the Nazis in Italy, and liberated southern France? Now the presence of these brave soldiers has been removed by racist generals and denied a rightful place in the military history of the liberation of Paris."

Big Rant had hastily created two hand puppets with an oversized black sock named Georges Dukson, and a dirty white sock named Whitey Dwighty. She enacted the relevant tone of voice for both puppets in a short parley.

> WHITEY: War and liberation have always been white.
>
> DUKSON: *La Résistance* was never your white liberation.
>
> WHITEY: Move aside for our history of combat soldiers.
>
> DUKSON: Whitey Dwighty is out of step with liberty.

Poesy May Fairbanks had rescued two books of poems by Robert Frost, *A Further Range* and *A Witness Tree*, from the ruins of the Nibwaakaa Library, but that worthy gesture alone would not save the great New England poet from the mockery of his slow reading of "The Gift Outright" at the inauguration of John F. Kennedy. The inaugural audience was enchanted by his august stature and wispy white hair in the cold wind, but his politics of

poetry and exclusion of a native presence on the land only served the same
fascist separatism of federal policies. Poesy lowered her voice and slowly
mocked the first two lines and the last two lines of "The Gift Outright."

> *The land was ours before we were the land's*
> *We grabbed the land and made it ours*
> *She was our land more than a hundred years*
> *Pious pilgrims landed on biblical time*
>
> . . . .
>
> *But still unstoried, artless, unenhanced*
> *The land was enriched with native dream songs*
> *Such as she was, such as she will become*
> *This continent is our totemic creation story*

"Robert Frost recited that poem of fraudulent sentiments and nothing
more at the inauguration," chanted Poesy May. "This land is native land,
and natives are the true storiers of the land, not the threadbare yarns of colonial pillagers and churchy deliverance."

"Never a nostalgic dumping ground," wrote Dummy.

"Natives are the creative storiers of natural motion and totemic unions
with animals, and our dream songs are in the clouds not at wistful inaugura-
tions," said Big Rant.

"The Gift Outright" was protected by copyright, "a forged literary treaty,
and that was another good reason to mock the pious images of a poetic land
grab," said Basile.

"Treaties are everlasting ironies," said La Chance.

Dummy, Prometheus, and By Now sauntered to the post office with the
four mongrels on Monday, January 23, 1961, a cold morning three days after
the literary plunder of native land by Robert Frost and the inauguration of
President John F. Kennedy. The snow was lumpy and crusted and the bitter
wind swished in the trees. Rowdy ravens were perched in the birch trees,
and the cardinals whistled in the white pine. The downy woodpeckers were
elusive, a slight whinny in the distance. Blue Jays whirred and scolded the
clouds, and other birds celebrated the morning with distinctive songs. The
owls were poised and silent. Dummy was convinced that dream songs and
the winter revelry of ravens countered the snow ghosts that so easily seduced lonesome natives with cruel rumors of hope, shame, and pity.

The post office was a cozy winter sanctuary, and there were always natives gathered around the space heater. Postcard Mary handed over an
oversized postcard addressed to Basile Hudon Beaulieu from Nathan
Crémieux, owner of the Galerie Ghost Dance in Paris.

"Aloysius, Basile, By Now, Prometheus: The Ghost Shirts captivate visitors, but we need more of your art and literature. Eager to plan an exposition of *Totemic Chance* by Aloysius and publish new stories by Basile. Paris
remembers your native irony and hand puppets that tease the *Gendarmerie
nationale*. Charles de Gaulle was elected the President of France. Plan to
visit White Earth Reservation first week of June on my way to the Century
21 Exposition in Seattle, Washington, in July and August. We must meet at
Tilikum Place, July 4, 1962, in the morning, ten days before Bastille Day."

Postcard Mary circulated a sensational hearsay version of the postcard
within a few days. "President Charles de Gaulle, Basile, and Aloysius
teased the Paris police with totemic art and hand puppets and later they
plan to capture thousands of tourists in a Spacecraft at the Seattle World's
Fair dressed in sacred Ghost Dance Shirts."

Basile waved the postcard, looked away in silence, and then proclaimed
that the troupe of puppeteers and mongrels were on the way to the Fair in
Seattle. The mongrels sensed an adventure and barked, bayed, and danced
in circles. Dummy worried the mongrels would not be allowed on the train
and printed a firm declaration on the inside chalk board, "No train, no
mongrels, no puppets, no show in Seattle."

Aloysius searched recent newspaper advertisements for buses and
campers and located a 1949 REO School Bus for sale in nearby Detroit
Lakes. The final price was negotiated to include a rebuilt engine, new brake
linings, and new tires to secure the expedition through four states and over
the Rocky Mountains to the Exposition in Seattle.

Big Rant and Bad Boy painted two names in bold letters on both sides of
the bus, *Theatre of Chance* and *Célébrité de Rien*, or Celebrity of Nothing.
They also painted the same names on the turn signal arms. The left turn
signal was *Theatre of Chance*, and *Célébrité de Rien* was the right turn signal. The school bus was built to safely transport forty-two students, and ten
double seats were converted to narrow bunks. A water tank and chemical
toilet were installed, and the back four windows were blackened for privacy.

The troupe agreed to create hand puppets and scenes of colloquies on the road and present special puppet parleys at the World's Fair. Poesy May declared she would fashion cloth hand puppets that depicted Robert Frost and Chief Seattle and create ironic poetic lines for a parley.

Master Jean created a huge canvas puppet that depicted the theoretical physicist and Big Brother of hydrogen bombs, Edward Teller. The other hand puppet he created was slender and made of rough calico with painted waves, and represented the entire crew of sailors on the *Diago Fukuryu Maru*, a fishing boat named the Lucky Dragon. The twenty-three sailors were exposed to radioactive ashes and mysterious white rain from Castle Bravo, a thermonuclear weapon tested at Bikini Atoll, and a thousand times more intense than Little Boy that destroyed the city of Hiroshima and Fat Man that destroyed the city of Nagasaki.

Truman La Chance created four fantastic puppets with two broken beavertail canoe paddles and roughly depicted the outline of totemic beaver, bear, wolf, and sandhill crane on the blades of the paddles. He turned the paddle faces and the mongrels cocked their heads and moaned. The only comeback bay was from Trophy Bay.

Aloysius celebrated the spirit of beavertail paddle puppets and created on paper bags the caricatures of John F. Kennedy and Sitting Bull, the Lakota resistance leader, Tallulah Bankhead, the actress, and Sacagawea, the Shoshone woman who directed the celebrated Lewis and Clark Expedition. The caricatures painted on each side of the brown bags were easy puppet parleys by the turn of a paddle, and one puppeteer could turn the caricatures of puppet faces and present the creative talk back of four puppets. Bad Boy created the script from selected quotations by President Kennedy and Sitting Bull. Big Rant created the puppet parley of Tallulah Bankhead and Sacagawea from actual excerpts.

> KENNEDY: We are the heirs of that first revolution.
> SITTING BULL: Love of possessions is a disease with them.
> KENNEDY: Both sides explore what problems unite us.
> SITTING BULL: Go back home where you came from.
> KENNEDY: Ask not what your country can do for you.
> SITTING BULL: Not necessary that eagles should be crows.

TALLULAH: Only good girls keep diaries.

SACAGAWEA: Everything I do is for my people.

TALLULAH: Bad girls don't have the time.

SACAGAWEA: Everything I do is for my people.

TALLULAH: My heart is as pure as the driven slush.

SACAGAWEA: Everything I do is for my people.

Dummy packed the Silvertone hand crank record player, *Madama Butterfly*, *La Bohème*, and opera recordings, clothes, bandanas, and that last night at Spirit Lake she read selections from *The Essays of Michel de Montaigne*. She copied several selections in a notebook as usual and then directed Big Rant to read out loud a single paragraph early the next morning as the *Theatre of Chance* bus slowly departed for Seattle.

Big Rant recited the selection from Michel de Montaigne, "We are never at home, we are always beyond. Fear, desire, hope, project us toward the future and steal from us the consideration of what is, to busy us with what will be, even when we shall no longer be." Aloysius drove the bus to the post office, and the troupe cheered, and the mongrels bayed.

9

STRAY SHADOWS

The *Theatre of Chance* was loaded with food, books, puppets, clothes, cooking utensils, camp chairs, and a portable stove. The troupe of resistance storiers and stowaways selected rows on the bus early in the morning, and the five loyal mongrels panted and bayed with excitement in the front seats.

Dummy carried Sitting Bull the hand puppet in a velvet pouch over her shoulder. She secretly carved from fallen birch the stately countenance of the Hunkpapa Lakota spiritual leader, resistance visionary, and solemn warrior who defended native sovereignty, envisioned the defeat of the Seventh Cavalry at the Battle of the Little Big Horn, and encouraged the peace and solace of the Ghost Dance Religion. Sitting Bull was always ready to be honored in a puppet parley, and she carried two rough blocks of fallen birch to create other puppets on the road.

Big Rant read out loud a quotation from Wovoka, or Jack Wilson, the great vision of the Ghost Dance Religion. "When the sun died, I went up to heaven and saw god and all the people who had died a long time ago," shouted Big Rant. They "told me to come back and tell my people they must be good and love one another, and not fight, or steal, or lie." Wovoka was granted a "dance to give to my people."

The Ghost Dance vision was translated into several native languages and circulated more directly in English by the first native graduates from mission and federal boarding schools. "All the dead men will come back to life again," was an easy message delivered on ordinary postcards to desolate natives on treaty reservations with post offices. The revolution of a sacred dance was revealed in visionary heart stories and through the hearsay of postcards. "Their spirits will come to their bodies again," and all natives "must dance, everywhere keep on dancing."

"Dance is the natural motion of a vision," said By Now.

Master Jean raised the bugle and played a concise version of the Last

Post. Daniel cocked an ear and delivered a clear mellow moan, and the other mongrels carried on with harmonic bays.

Dummy posted a stay at bay notice on the cabin door and carried two chalk boards, one for dream songs and the other for hearsay and directions. She created a dream song to celebrate her first journey outside the reservation since the Great Hinckley Fire.

spirit lake memories
puppets and loyal mongrels
theatre of chance in natural motion
heart stories and parleys
liberty on the road

Postcard Mary imagined the necessary departure hearsay that Monday, June 25, 1962. "Spaceships landed on a tower at the Seattle World's Fair and lured notable visitors from France, Spain, Germany, Italy, Russia, the United Kingdom, and the White Earth Reservation to wait, wait, wait, and hear curious stories about the totemic ghost dance of beaver, otter, bear, and other animals from the ancient fur trade, a wild puppet parley of stray shadows and the bay of loyal mongrels on Bastille Day."

"Waiting for totemic ghost dancers," shouted By Now.

"Waiting for the hearsay of ravens," said Big Rant.

"Waiting for totemic solidarity," wrote Dummy.

"Waiting for the Baron of Patronia," said Prometheus.

"Waiting for stories of tragic irony," said Bad Boy.

"Waiting for native heart stories," wrote Dummy.

"Waiting for puppet parleys," said Master Jean.

"Waiting for the trickster of liberty," shouted By Now.

"Waiting for Sitting Bull," wrote Dummy.

"Waiting for Hole in the Day," said Basile.

"Waiting for Wovoka," whispered Poesy May.

"Waiting for totemic chance," said Aloysius.

"Waiting for nothing," said La Chance.

"Waiting for *célébrités de rien*," said Prometheus.

"Waiting for Samuel Beckett," said Basile.

The mongrels sensed a natural turn of native stories and raised their heads to moan and bay in the post office. Big John groaned and moved to the side. Tallulah delivered a beautiful early morning contralto bay as she bounced on her front paws, always ready to sing out with the other mongrels, and mainly with the mongrel coonhound Trophy Bay.

Dummy printed a dream song on a chalk board in response to the spaceship departure hearsay by Postcard Mary. George Eliot was at her side with a great soprano bay, and Dingleberry snorted, yodeled, and danced in circles.

postcard mary
creates marvelous worlds
waiting for heart stories
eternal ghosts of the fur trade
hearsay of liberty

Postcard Mary gave the stowaways undelivered copies of the local *Detroit Lakes Tribune* and the June 16, 1962 special edition of the *New Yorker* magazine with the first chapters of *Silent Spring* by Rachel Carson. Lastly, she handed over a box of books mailed to the stowaways by Harmony Baswewe, the generous librarian of the burned Library of Nibwaakaa. The books were published in the past few years, *Nobody Knows My Name* by James Baldwin, *Ishi in Two Worlds* by Theodora Kroeber, *The Divided Self* by R. D. Laing, *Zen in the Art of Archery* by Eugen Herrigel, *The Unnamable* and *Waiting for Godot* by Samuel Beckett, *Resistance, Rebellion, and Death* by Albert Camus, and *The Voyage of the Lucky Dragon* by Ralph Lapp.

Harmony explained in a letter that *Ishi in Two Worlds* was a gift for Prometheus, and *Resistance, Rebellion, and Death* was for those who served in the French Résistance. She suggested that Big Rant read out loud "The Discovery of What It Means to Be an American," the first chapter of *Nobody Knows My Name*, and the two short essays of the first chapter, "The Liberation of Paris," in *Resistance, Rebellion, and Death*. The first essay, "The Blood of Freedom" was first published in *Combat*, August 24, 1944, and the second, "The Night of Truth," on October 27, 1944.

By Now started the journey of the *Theatre of Chance* and turned north through Ogema, Waubun, and Mahnomen, and then near Bijou and the treaty border, Tallulah emerged from under a seat. The husky mongrel delivered a contralto bay and the other mongrels circled to bay in a chorus of tributes. By Now parked on the shoulder and read out loud the note that was attached to the blue floral bandana collar on the mongrel stowaway.

"Tallulah is a mongrel descendant of the great brassy women of the movies, and she never holds back charm, worries, or contralto bays around other mongrels," wrote Postcard Mary. "Yes, she barks and bays at many reservation melds that visit the post office, but she is more excited in the company of Trophy Bay. Tallulah waits for his visits at the post office, and then, as you know, she runs away with him to Spirit Lake. Trophy Bay and Tallulah have earned the right to be together, and now especially with the stowaways and puppets on the way to the World's Fair. There is a case of her favorite dog food under one of the seats."

"Tallulah is a stowaway mongrel," shouted Bad Boy.

"Trophy Bay bays and she stays," said Poesy May.

"Tallulah knows how to read the bays," said Big Rant.

"Trophy Bay is a lucky coonhound," said La Chance.

"Daniel waits to bay with Tallulah," said Master Jean.

By Now turned west onto Highway 2 toward Grand Forks, North Dakota, across the Red River, and the ten native voyagers and six mongrels camped that first night near Devils Lake, the curse of a slack translation. The lake was named *mni wakan*, or spirit water, on native land of the Dakota. The mongrels rushed out of the bus and plunged into the Spirit Water.

The stray shadows on the drift prairie wavered in natural motion as the bus clattered on the rough highway through Minot, the Magic City and Air Force Base, to Williston, North Dakota. The troupe camped the second night on the Missouri River near Wolf Point on the Fort Peck Indian Reservation in Montana.

The *Theatre of Chance* was parked near the great river, and as the sun slowly reached into the night the bus became a silhouette, the mongrel shadows a trickster scene, and the troupe of natives gathered on the riverbank to create a second round of heart stories on the road.

Polaris, Venus, Arcturus, and many other bright stars shimmered on the slow dark river, and the emotive voice in the distance was Elvis Presley singing, "Are You Lonesome Tonight." George Eliot soughed at the end of the popular song, the river was silent, and no one in the troupe was lonesome that glorious night on the Missouri River.

Poesy May envisioned the native names of constellations, Perseus, *as-iniikaa*, or stone, Hercules, *miskwi*, or blood, and Ursa Major, *makoons*, or bear cub, and then she continued to whisper the names of great natives in the clouds, Hole in the Day, Crazy Horse, Pocahontas, Chief Joseph, Geronimo, Sitting Bull, Standing Bear, Tecumseh, Sacagawea, Chief Seattle, and Louis Riel.

Fort Peck natives were curious about the names on the bus, and one elder related that native creation stories were "tricksters of chance parked on a reservation." By Now was ready for a night of bright stories and mockery and placed the rickety camp chairs near the river. Her tease of one native elder at the river was slight, "So many good stories with chancy women."

Bracer, a young native woman, declared that she was a competitive archer. She wore a wrist guard and boasted about training to compete in the World Archery Federation. "Natives always live better when the games are authentic traditions."

"Archery is natural motion, not a show of wrist guards or deadeye competition," said Master Jean. "Stationary targets are never true or secure, never accurate, and never a reason to boast about traditions."

The Fort Peck natives were silent at first, either to embrace, evade, or tease the notions of archery, traditions, competition, and targets in a single sentence. Dingleberry sneezed and bounced in the grass. George Eliot groaned, and other mongrels turned away in silence and waded in the river. The sweet scent of tobacco was in the air, and nothing more mattered that night than the steady natural motion of the Missouri River.

"Ghost stories in the great river," wrote Dummy.

Basile was hesitant to court conversations about native cultures or traditions as a visitor from another reservation, but that night, almost lost in the tobacco smoke, he told a story about a native man with a heavily scarred face who blamed the rage of bears for the wounds. The native said the scars were more than chance or nothing, the bear scars were the shame of the fur trade, and he counted out the claw marks on his face. The marks were steady, evenly spaced, and not the claw marks that a hungry bear would make on the face of a native.

The native was haunted by bears and created the scars one by one over several years in prison for the theft of money, rifles, jewelry, and a taxidermy mounted bear from a rich rancher and trophy hunter who lived alone in a modern mansion of stuffed animals on a dirt road cul-de-sac in the mountains. The burglar and rancher were never seen as stray shadows or celebrities of nothing, they were rather the poachers and poseurs of nothing. One was razor marked with stupidity, and the rancher was a moneyed predator forever shamed for his taxidermy trophies.

Master Jean countered the custom of taxidermy with strange stories about a shaman who staged a circle of mummies near his wigwam, but the hideous scenes never scared away the poseurs and greedy hunters. The seven mummies were rescued from a ditch of unnamed city paupers and decorated with the names of totemic animals, Beaver, Muskrat, Otter, Bear, Mink, and Wolf. The mummies with totemic names were shot by hunters in every season of vengeance.

Dummy sat in the back of the bus and read the first chapter of *Zen in the Art of Archery* by Eugen Herrigel. Trophy Bay and Tallulah were at her side. Poesy May sat nearby and whispered several lines of Vladimir and Estragon from *Waiting for Godot* by Samuel Beckett. The sweet smoke and stories lasted deep into the night on the Missouri River.

The *Theatre of Chance* was on the road early the next morning when the air was thin and cooler and arrived late in the afternoon in Browning, Montana. Dummy printed a dream song on a chalk board about distance and elevation.

reservation passage
natives of fort peck and browning
higher than white earth
mongrels and stowaways
stories in thin air

Aloysius parked the bus in a public campground near the Museum of the Plains Indian on the Blackfeet Indian Reservation, and with a spectacular view of the Rocky Mountains. Naturally the troupe visited the museum galleries and admired the diverse ceremonial headdresses, original murals, buffalo robes, weapons, quilled shirts, bows, and other movables of the Blackfeet, Crow, Northern Cheyenne, and eight other native cultures.

Dummy was captivated by the selection of traditional bows and quivers of the Northern Cheyenne and Blackfeet on display in the museum. She heard the worried bark of the mongrels but returned to the same display several times to imagine the native stories of the carved curve of the bows.

Dummy paused to envision every bow on display, and the loyal mongrels waited outside the museum until a pack of nasty wild dogs chased the mongrels back to the *Theatre of Chance*. Hail Mary and George Eliot growled and barked from the safety of the bus, and Dingleberry flashed her tiny teeth, yelped, and yodeled at the wild hounds of the museum.

By Now and Prometheus secretly visited a native trading post and bought Dummy a bow and quiver with arrows crafted by an elder of the Northern Cheyenne. The bow was about four feet high and carved from mountain juniper. The leather quiver was decorated with glass beads and the six arrows were fletched with turkey feathers.

Dummy was surprised with the solemn presentation of the bow and quiver, and wiped tears from her cheeks. She tested at once the bow and arrows on a burlap bag target stuffed with straw. The first two arrows were wide of the target, and the last two arrows hit the center. The troupe was silent and wisely avoided any gestures of praise as they gathered around the campfire that night to eat beans, boiled eggs, and wild rice and created trickster stories about long and short bows. Dummy printed a dream song on a chalk board about the bow and quiver of arrows.

juniper bow
quiver of carved arrows
horseback and heart stories
clouds in natural motion
chase of native liberty

By Now told the story about the trickster who shot himself into the mountains with a giant cedar bow. The native trickster carved the bow to hunt down demons, but the arrows were never carved true or fast enough. At first, the demons were disguised as missionaries and pitched twigs in the air and mocked the stories about tricksters. Only a native trickster could silence the demons of disease and poseurs of tradition.

The demons were everywhere, in every native scene and sorrow, and dithered in the ordinary with delight, always ready to take advantage of the slightest sentiments of hope, shame, feigned weakness, or sense of destiny.

The demons lingered in memory and waited in the disguise of churchy elders, birds of prey, and fascist federal agents.

Native shamans beat hand drums and create strange songs to distract the dreadful demons, and at the same time tricksters listen to their relations the stones and fashion a giant cedar bow. The bow was more than twice the height of an ordinary native hunter, so the trickster braced the bow stave between two birch trees and pulled and pushed the woven bow string. The trickster lost his stance as he strained to shoot an arrow, and by chance the taut bow string shot the woodland trickster into the mountains.

The trickster returned a few months later disguised as a coyote one day, a field mouse with huge ears on another day, a blue raven for a few days, and as a hungry mongrel on other days. The demons were easily weakened with laughter over the stories of the native trickster who shot himself into the mountains as an arrow.

One night the trickster teased the demons with the shimmer of a campfire and then lured the bent demons one by one into the flames, and they were caught forever in campfires. The frantic demons lasted as wavers, sneers, and the twisted faces of tinder fires and only escaped long enough to light a cigarette, or flash with vengeance in forest fires, or cause a blaze of books at the Library of Nibwaakaa.

The *Theatre of Chance* was on the highway at dawn the next morning. Aloysius drove the bus west near Calf Robe Mountain, Little Dog Mountain, and Marias Pass Obelisk at more than five thousand feet above sea level. The mongrels were perched in the front seats and watched the curves of the Flathead River to West Glacier. Snow covered the great mountains on each side of the highway to Columbia Falls and Kalispell. Naturally, there was a sense of adventure and romance about the towns that emerged around a curve on a mountain road, the tease of nature, natural motion, the meander of a river, and the people who lived in the splendor of a marvelous landscape.

The *Theatre of Chance* was in slow motion on the highway, no more than fifty miles an hour. Campers, cars, and trucks passed the bus, and children smiled and waved at the mongrels in the front seats. Dummy sometimes gestured that a car with children was about to pass, and the troupe crouched in the seats and raised hand puppets to pose in the bus windows.

Aloysius parked the bus near the Kootenai River Falls about fifteen miles west of Libby. The river roared in the thin air, and the birds and stray shadows swayed with the trees on the rocky shoreline. The Kootenai or Kutenai natives consider the river and waterfall the great heart of the world, a sacred place, and forever the steady course of the mighty river was the sound of natural motion and creation.

Big Rant shouted a warning as the mongrels bounded down to the river. The rush of water over the rocks was not secure, and the mongrels could easily be caught in the fast currents. Trophy Bay and Tallulah were cautious and waded in the shallow pools of glacial water from the mountains. Hail Mary rolled over in the cold shallows and then meandered back to the bus. Dingleberry shivered and sneezed at the edge of the river. Master Jean and Daniel the spaniel mongrel walked slowly down the river and counted the flash of fish in the rapids.

Dummy climbed on a smooth boulder near the shore and searched for rainbow trout or water ouzels in the river. Her white hair waved in the wind, strand by strand, a natural scene that might have caught the eye of blue ravens, bald eagles, black bears, mountain elk, or grey wolves at a distance. She closely watched the river for more than an hour, counted the number of water ouzels, and pointed once toward the mountain and seven times at the river and wrote a dream song on the chalk board.

water ouzels
stray shadows in the river
rush of memories
glacial traces in the stone
kootenai creation

Sandpoint, Idaho, was the destination the fourth night on the road. The *Theatre of Chance* parked close to the Pend Oreille River and the stowaways prepared a dinner of rice, red beans, cheddar cheese, and carrots, and later the troupe gathered around the campfire to stay warm. Big Rant read short sections of the first chapter of *Nobody Knows My Name* by James Baldwin, and the native back talk version was recited by Bad Boy and Basile.

"I left America because I doubted my ability to survive the fury of the color problem here," Big Rant read out loud over the campfire. "I wanted to prevent myself from becoming *merely* a Negro; or, even, merely a Negro writer. I wanted to find out in what way the *specialness* of my experience could be made to connect me with other people instead of dividing me from them."

"I left home on the reservation because of a violent uncle and could not survive the fever and fury of his drunken rage," said Bad Boy. "I wanted to prevent myself from becoming the prey of the snow ghosts or merely a suicidal native reader of the burned pages of Aristotle. I wanted to find out in what way my native experience could be made to connect me with other people, authors, and books instead of dividing me from dream songs and libraries."

Big Rant read slowly, "The American writer, in Europe, is released, first of all, from the necessity of apologizing for himself. It is not until he *is* released from the habit of flexing his muscles and proving that he is just a 'regular guy' that he realizes how crippling this habit has been. It is not necessary for him, there, to pretend to be something he is not, for the artist does not encounter in Europe the same suspicion he encounters here."

Basile related that "native writers and artists in Paris are released from the necessity of apologizing or pretending to prove that they are just regular guys because the native artist does not encounter in Paris the same suspicions, abuses, and judgments of inferiority he encounters in America."

Big Rant moved closer to the fire and continued to read a section from *Nobody Knows My Name*, "The charge has often been made against American writers that they do not describe society, and have no interest in it. They only describe individuals in opposition to it, or isolated from it. Of course, what the American writer is describing is his own situation."

Basile related a native version, "The charge has often been made against native writers that they do not describe tradition and have no interest in it. They only describe individuals in opposition to it, or isolated from it. Of course, what the native writer is describing is his own creative situation and resistance to scenes of cultural absence and victimry."

"Not many native writers were slaves," said Master Jean.

"Not many natives were authors," said Big Rant.

Bad Boy declared that he was the situational native storier of the night and would create descriptions of the fantastic exploits of the philosopher Aristotle who once mocked native shamans and tent shakers at La Pointe on Madeline Island in Lake Superior. "Aristotle was an heir of the fur trade and created the imitation of action in the theatre of tragedy, but when he mocked the native shamans and tent shakers for the imitations and stagey travesties, the great philosopher was turned into a totemic blue raven and the tease of natural motion in literature."

Master Jean readied a beavertail paddle for another puppet parley on the road with Aristotle and James Baldwin. Aloysius painted caricatures of the two paddle puppets on each side of a small paper bag. Bad Boy selected quotations from the burned books by Aristotle and Big Rant selected sentences and phrases from *Nobody Knows My Name* by James Baldwin.

The troupe and mongrels gathered around the campfire to hear the puppet parley as the paddle turned from one caricature to the other, Aristotle to Baldwin, and back again. Master Jean turned the paddle and Bad Boy was the voice of Aristotle. Big Rant was the steady mellow voice of James Baldwin.

ARISTOTLE: For nobility is excellence of race.

BALDWIN: Any real change implies the breakup of the world.

ARISTOTLE: And poverty is the parent of revolution and crime.

BALDWIN: The interior life is a real life.

ARISTOTLE: There is no genius without some touch of madness.

BALDWIN: Intangible dreams of people have a tangible effect.

ARISTOTLE: You will never do anything without courage.

BALDWIN: Every society is governed by hidden laws.

ARISTOTLE: For man, when perfected, is the best of animals.

BALDWIN: Men do not like to be protected, it emasculates them. This is what the black men know, it is the reality they have lived with; it is what white men do not want to know.

ARISTOTLE: I count him braver who overcomes his desires than him who conquers his enemies; for the hardest victory is the victory over self.

BALDWIN: People are continually pointing out to me the wretchedness of white people in order to console me for the wretchedness of blacks. But an itemized account of the American failure does not console me and it should not console anyone else.

ARISTOTLE: The worst form of inequality is to try to make unequal things equal.

BALDWIN: There are few things under heaven more unnerving than the silent, accumulating contempt and hatred of a people.

ARISTOTLE: It is not enough to win a war; it is more important to organize the peace.

BALDWIN: The things that most white people imagine that they can salvage from the storm of life is really, in sum, their innocence. It was this commodity precisely which I had to get rid of at once, literally, on pain of death.

ARISTOTLE: The soul never thinks without a picture.

BALDWIN: The artistic image is not intended to represent the thing itself, but, rather, the reality of the forces the thing contains.

ARISTOTLE: Nature, there is something of the marvelous.

BALDWIN: Whether I like it or not, or whether you like it or not, we are bound together forever. We are part of each other.

ARISTOTLE: The aim of the wise is not to secure pleasure, but to avoid pain. To avoid criticism say nothing, do nothing, be nothing.

"Aristotle is buried forever with ancient books, and never noticed that by declaring nothing as a *célébrité de rien* he could reserve irony but never avoid criticism," said Prometheus. "He might have avoided the timeworn custody of philosophy, the tragedy of pleasure, praise, shame, hope and poesy, equality, and remain a genius as an ironic celebrity of nothing."

"Aristotle was an imitation of tragedy," said Bad Boy.

"Aristotle could have been a native," said Master Jean.

"Aristotle could have been a shaman," said Big Rant.

"Aristotle was a deadeye archer with stray shadows, and he has hit the targets of autocracies and cultural dominion, shame, and the aesthetics of vanity for more than two thousand years," said Bad Boy.

Trophy Bay raised his head and delivered a mellow bay, and Tallulah bounced on her front paws and bayed in harmony. Master Jean removed the brown bag puppet faces from the canoe paddle and the other mongrels raised their heads to bay and moan with pleasure. Dingleberry snorted and yodeled as she danced around the campfire.

By Now drove the *Theatre of Chance* slowly along the Pend Oreille River to Newport, Spokane, and then west to Davenport, Almira, and Coulee City to the Columbia River near Sunnyslope, Washington, the perfect destination on the fifth day, Friday, June 29, 1962.

Big Rant read out loud the first chapter of *Silent Spring* by Rachel Carson on the road between Sandpoint and Sunnyslope. La Chance listened to the entire reading on the bus and created an original parley between Rachel Carson with her actual words and Migizi, a bald eagle, two voices that represented the human and totemic casualties of contemporary chemical cultures. La Chance was the mellow voice of Migizi, the courageous bald eagle, and Big Rant was the solemn and heartfelt voice of Rachel Carson, the marine biologist, conservationist, and author of *Silent Spring*.

> CARSON: Spring without voices, no dawn chorus of robins.
> MIGIZI: No dream songs with so many poisoned suckers.
> CARSON: One spring, a strange blight crept over the area.
> MIGIZI: A deadly curse that poisoned the water and fish.
> CARSON: Mysterious maladies swept the flocks of chickens.
> MIGIZI: The seasons were never the same for birds and animals.
> CARSON: Everywhere was the shadow of death.
> MIGIZI: The shadows of shame over our nests in the red pine.
> CARSON: Farmers told of much illness among their families.
> MIGIZI: The water and fish were poisoned with insecticides.
> CARSON: New chemicals come in an endless stream.
> MIGIZI: Loons and eagles, delicate eggs and empty nests.
> CARSON: Dangerous chemicals from birth to death.
> MIGIZI: Gasping fish washed ashore on the rivers.
> CARSON: The people had done it to themselves.
> MIGIZI: Totemic birds and animals were decimated twice.
> CARSON: Pollution had rapidly become almost universal.
> MIGIZI: First in the fur trade and then the chemical trade.
> CARSON: Radiation has changed the nature of the world.
> MIGIZI: Bald eagles soar in clouds of nuclear radiation.

George Eliot, Daniel, and Dingleberry sat next to Dummy during the parley and sensed the serious tones of voice. Daniel raised his head with a hesitant bark and generous bay. Dummy was distraught about the chemical mercenaries and praised the parley about the bald eagles. Big Rant read out loud a dream song by Dummy.

bald eagles
poisoned by suckers
chemical traders
lethal summer sprays
lakes of graves

The fifth night on the road the native troupe and mongrels gathered around a campfire, and after dinner the ironic stories about tricksters and travel adventures easily turned to teasing. Dummy was the center of the teases that night because she had concentrated the entire day on the slow draw, target meditation, and the perfect moment to release of the bow string. She read *Zen in the Art of Archery* and imagined the scenes described by Eugen Herrigel. Big Rant was instructed in the usual chalk board messages to read out loud several paragraphs from the book.

"As in the case of archery, there can be no question but that these arts are ceremonies. More clearly than the teacher could express it in words, they tell the pupil that the right frame of mind for the artist is only reached when the preparing and the creating, the technical and the artistic, the material and the spiritual, the project and the object, flow together without a break," read Big Rant. "The important thing is that an inward movement is thereby initiated. The teacher pursues it, and, without influencing its course with further instructions which would merely disturb it, helps the pupil in the most secret and intimate way he knows, by direct transference of the spirit, as it is called in Buddhist circles."

Master Jean centered his meditation as an archer on natural motion, not on a statue or the favor of stationary targets. Dummy created her own intuitive course of movement as an archer. She pictured the entire archer, bow, arrow, and target together in natural motion.

The archer, the custom, and the artist are one. "The art of the inner work, which unlike the outer does not forsake the artist which the artist does not 'do' and can only 'be,' springs from depths of which the day knows nothing," related Big Rant.

Dummy encouraged Big Rant to read more creatively the selections from *Zen in the Art of Archery*, and so she deleted or substituted the heavy pronouns of gender. Dummy wrote on the chalk board that there were "stray totemic shadows of natural motion in the art of native archery."

Tallulah raised her head, turned to the side and delivered a marvelous contralto bay. The other mongrels once again bayed in harmony. Dummy placed the burlap straw target a short distance from the campfire. She drew the first arrow, paused to respect the ambiguity of native creation stories, concentrated on the memory of the feathers, the curve and tension of the mountain juniper bow, the natural motion of the arrow, and then without a sense of cause, motivation, or constraint the arrow turned slowly in the air and reached the center of the target.

Dummy was a close and creative reader with a visionary sense of presence, and her silence, perception, and unreserved concentration revealed moments of curious liberty. She wrote on the chalk board, "the art of archery is a native dream song, stray arrows in the clouds." She released five more arrows directly into the heart of the burlap target.

> *the way of archery*
> *meditation and natural motion*
> *arrows and dream songs*
> *silence of stray shadows*
> *native chance*

Prometheus drove the *Theatre of Chance* through the great Cascade Mountains along the Wenatchee River to Cashmere and Leavenworth, and then along Nason Creek to Stevens Pass and the Tye River to Skykomish and along the Skykomish River to Sulton, Monroe, Everett, and then he turned south on Highway 99 to Seattle and the World's Fair. The Space Needle was visible at a great distance. The *Theatre of Chance* parked overnight near Pioneer Square.

10

NOAH LE GROS

Prometheus parked the *Theatre of Chance* overnight on James Street near the ruins of the Hotel Seattle in Pioneer Square, once the heart of the timber city, and about two miles from the Space Needle and the World's Fair.

Tallulah and Trophy Bay strayed and bayed near the Tlingit Totem Pole and the derelict Iron Pergola, and later they trotted along with La Chance, Bad Boy, and Big Rant to Pier 54 at the end of Spring Street. Puget Sound wooden steamers once called at the old dock when it was Pier 3, and some of the lonesome men on the street told stories about the busy merchants and the boisterous sale of fresh produce, poultry, bundles of rhubarb, potatoes, and the memorable clank, clank, clank of heavy metal milk cans.

Hail Mary trotted in the opposite direction with Basile and Aloysius to the top of the hill with a view of the bay on Yesler Way. By Now and Prometheus wandered around the old brick buildings at Pioneer Square. Poesy May and Master Jean stayed on the bus to work on scripts for the puppet parleys, and Daniel sat in the front seat and pretended to be vigilant. Dummy read *The Voyage of the Lucky Dragon* by Ralph Lapp and made notes for Master Jean.

George Eliot and Dingleberry stayed close to the bus and were easily shied by the heavy and uneven tread of hungry men who had endured a pioneer culture of greed and debris in the ruins of timber chutes and civilization. Some of the men were combat veterans, and some no doubt were the lonesome native heirs of the Duwamish who once lived on the nearby bay for thousands of years before the predatory explorers and possessive outlanders named it Elliott Bay.

Basile raised both arms in front of the Tlingit Totem Pole and shouted that the pole was a memorial to greed and depredation. The veterans winced, the mongrels were shied by the temper, and the stowaways waited in silence for an explanation. "The first pole was cut down and stolen from a native village on the coast of Alaska more than sixty years ago by predatory members of the Chamber of Commerce, and then the great standard of totemic relations was vandalized by an arsonist."

Dummy slowly circled the totem pole with the mongrels, and then bowed, she wrote later, "to the stature of traditional native hearsay."

"The burned pole could not be restored, so politicians paid cash to Tlingit carvers to create this new ironic totemic money pole to restore the conceit of Pioneer Square," said Basile.

"City totems must be ironic," said Master Jean.

"Necessary mockery of relations," wrote Dummy.

"Totemic political relations," said Bad Boy.

"The course of civilization," said La Chance.

"Public declarations of vanity," shouted By Now.

"City totems of sanctimony," said Aloysius.

Daniel nudged two weary men to the bus, one was short with a great white beard and used a gnarled boxelder walking stick, and the other was bald and peaky. The man with the beard had a strong voice and revealed that he was a combat veteran of the American Expeditionary Force and was twice decorated for his bravery and wounds in the First World War.

"Honor the down and out war veterans at the broken heart of the city," said By Now. She placed camp chairs near the bus and invited the two men to a meager meal of rice, beans, and a boiled egg. She teased and healed with native stories and at the same time patched minor wounds, soothed bruised feet and chafed skin with olive oil, and revealed that she once served as a nurse in *La Résistance* during the Nazi Occupation of France.

"War stories of compassion," said Prometheus.

"Heart stories of deadly combat," said Basile.

Toothy, an ironic nickname, told emotive stories about the suicidal hunger during the war, the haunted blue faces of scared mothers and silent children on the road, the absence of a single bird song in the gray mornings of war, and the deadly trench strategies determined over tea by secure commanders in tight polished boots.

By Now listened closely to the creative ventures of combat stories after more than forty years since the Great War. Toothy paused and then related that he shared a few boiled eggs and a small tin of monkey meat with seven other soldiers over more than two days in the steady cold rain and under constant enemy bombardments, and with a wistful smile he mentioned the raw, muddy, bloody faces of fear that spring in the fierce and deadly Battle of Château-Thierry.

Atomic 16, a curious nickname derived from a chemical element and the pungent traces of sulfur and charcoal in the nuclear ruins of Hiroshima, was almost bald with only thin patches of long rusty hair. He was bony, gray, badly blotched, and sickly, but cocked his head smartly and with a smile almost shouted his gratitude for the simple courtesy of a camp chair, a meal, and the chance to convey stories. Daniel moaned, moved closer, and rested his chin on the thigh of the soldier, the same signature gesture that embraced the stowaways.

Toothy was a wounded veteran of the First World War, and Atomic 16 was an infantry soldier who survived the ferocious combat in New Guinea, Leyte, and Luzon during the Second World War only to be poisoned by radiation when the army division carried out the first occupation and cleanup duties in Hiroshima.

Little Boy destroyed the port city on August 6, 1945, and nine days later the combat duties of war ended with the surrender of the Emperor of Japan. The war stories of two wounded veterans merged into the remembrance of combat desperation, absurdity, and comedy, and the stories of war never close with sentiments, historical surveys, or military duty dates.

Atomic 16 related that his nickname was directly connected to the journalist Wilfred Burchett, who commented on the vapors that "drifted from fissures in the soil and there was a dank, acrid, sulfurous smell." Corporal Samuel Hutson was teased with an atomic element nickname because for months he related countless scenes with the foreign correspondent.

"Burchett was the first journalist to report on the Atomic Plague in the ruins of Hiroshima," Atomic 16 told By Now. "He sat on burned chunks of radioactive concrete and created stories on a Hermes Baby Typewriter for the London *Daily Express*." Atomic 16 leaned forward in the camp chair and slowly recited from memory a paragraph from the story Burchett wrote for the newspaper. "In Hiroshima, thirty days after the first atomic bomb destroyed the city and shook the world, people are still dying, mysteriously and horribly, people who were uninjured in the cataclysm, from an unknown something which I can only describe as the Atomic Plague."

"Atomic 16 bears the atomic plague," said Toothy.

"Everyone was poisoned by radiation," said Aloysius.

"Thousands of soldiers were exposed to dangerous radiation in nuclear bomb tests at Yucca Flat in Nevada," said Basile. "The military used soldiers as guinea pigs, and government scientists proclaimed that radiation was not the cause of cancers."

"Radioactive iodine poisoned milk," said By Now.

"Break uranium and wither with cancer," said La Chance.

"Nuclear fission poisoned me as a soldier and now cursed as a new atomic creature with so many others of me poisoned with radiation," said Atomic 16.

"Fission in the blood," shouted Master Jean.

"Radiation memories," said La Chance.

"My genes have divided many times, more of me in the air, and there are many others of me on the streets, and we are the deadly shadows of nuclear war," said Atomic 16.

"Blue radioactive shadows," said Poesy May.

"The regret of me is in the eyes of others, and they know me, we are the same nuclear mutations," said Atomic 16.

"Nuclear totemic unions," said Bad Boy.

Dummy listened to the atomic stories with the mongrels George Eliot and Dingleberry at her side, and then she created a dream song about the atomic plague and ruins of a nuclear war on the chalk board. Later she mounted the dream song on the front bumper of the bus.

> *atomic plague*
> *deadly science overtakes poetry*
> *nuclear faces in a mirror*
> *ashes of children*
> *blue shadows of the dawn*

Nathan Crémieux named the date and place to meet but not the actual time. Paris was a culture of memorable places to meet, familiar parks and squares, but the precise time was vague in the easy count of social expectations. Nathan simply noted in his postcard that we were to meet at "Tilikum Place, July 4, 1962, in the morning."

The *Theatre of Chance* troupe and stowaways, along with Atomic 16 and Toothy and the six mongrels, set out early in the morning as a carnival parade to Tilikum Place, a cozy corner located about two blocks south of the landmark Space Needle at the World's Fair. Dummy worried about dog leash rules, so she loosely tied the mongrels together with red yarn to sidestep the fright of citizens and gaze of the police. Dingleberry circled, bounced, and bound her legs in yarn, but the other mongrels seemed to understand the restraint and willingly followed the pace of the puppeteer.

The Chief Seattle statue, Siahl or Seahl in the language of the Duwamish, was the obvious reason we were invited to meet at Tilikum Place. Aloysius pointed at the copper statue on a huge stone plinth and declared that the right arm was "no doubt raised as an ironic gesture of compromise with the explorers, territory government, and the loutish grunts of early loggers and settlers."

Chief Siahl, the principal of peace, apparently delivered a thoughtful, crucial, and elusive speech to honor Isaac Stevens, Commissioner of Indian Affairs of Washington Territory who visited the skid row timber town in 1854. Surely the visionary words of the native chief were heard in a native patois or trade language, and yet there were no reliable accounts of translation and how the wise words of the native leader endured for more than a century.

"The shadow words of a native," said Basile.

Doctor Henry Smith, the legislator and pioneer poet, as the story goes, created the prominent speech several years later from sketchy notes. Siahl was also known as Noah Le Gros. The first baptismal name was merged with a common nickname for one of the tallest natives in the local fur trade.

Poesy May created two husky cloth hand puppets and prepared for a morning parley near the copper statue of Chief Seattle. She raised the right arms of the puppets in front of the chiseled head of a bear on the face of the plinth and bounced the puppet heads from side to side to engage strays and strangers.

Prometheus wore white gloves and gestured to nearby tourists to move closer to the statue. About thirty people gathered around for the puppet parley of Chief Seattle, or Noah Le Gros, and the poet Robert Frost.

Poesy created ironic lines of the poem "The Gift Outright" for the hand puppet Robert Frost, and recast the strange poetic diction, "The land was ours before we were the land's," with the obvious, "We grabbed the land and made it ours." Frost recited in a frail voice the land was "still unstoried, artless, unenhanced" at the Inauguration of President John F. Kennedy.

The pleasant poet seemingly had no common sense of natives on the continent or the presence of other creation stories about the land.

Big Rant chanted the ironic recast lines of the poem by Robert Frost. Bad Boy was the mellow voice of the hand puppet Noah Le Gros and he pitched the serious poetic tones of the lines that were selected from his speech, the same words that were supposedly delivered more than a century ago.

LE GROS: My words are like the stars that never set.
FROST: We grabbed the land and made it ours.
LE GROS: Like the grass that covers the vast prairies.
FROST: Pious pilgrims landed here in biblical time.
LE GROS: While my people are few.
FROST: Even before we settled on the land.
LE GROS: I will not mourn over our untimely decay.
FROST: Mostly the states and rivers bear our names.
LE GROS: True it is, that revenge with our young braves.
FROST: True it is, we were only colonials on a boat.
LE GROS: Old men stay at home in times of war.
FROST: The pietists were celebrities of nothing.
LE GROS: Your god loves your people and hates mine.
FROST: Possessed by nothing but our declarations.
LE GROS: Two distinct races and must remain ever so.
FROST: We were weakened by holding back.
LE GROS: Our religion is the tradition of our ancestors.
FROST: We were weak about ourselves.
LE GROS: Our dead never forget the beautiful world.
FROST: No reason to hold back our customs.
LE GROS: Day and night cannot dwell together.
FROST: We surrendered and found salvation.
LE GROS: Men come and go like the waves of the sea.
FROST: We gave ourselves away outright.
LE GROS: Every part of this country is sacred to my people.
FROST: We conveyed only the feat of wars.
LE GROS: The white man will never be alone.
FROST: Forgetfully our catch was to the west.

LE GROS: Let him be just and deal kindly with my people.
FROST: The land with no stories was ours to enhance.
LE GROS: For the dead are not altogether powerless.
FROST: The land would never be lost in native memory.

Nathan Crémieux arrived at the very moment that the puppet Noah Le Gros declared, "Your god loves your people and hates mine." Poesy May raised the right arms of the two puppets, and the entire carnival of veterans, stowaways, and mongrels gathered around the owner of the *Galerie de la Danse des Esprits*, the Galerie Ghost Dance in Paris. Nathan praised the ironic lines created for the eminent native poet, and then raised his right arm, lowered his voice, and repeated the line, "Men come and go like the waves of the sea," in the words of the puppet Noah Le Gros.

"Le Gros was a slaver," shouted Master Jean.

"That should be in the parley," said La Chance.

"Slavery is not an irony," said Poesy May.

"Poetic slavers overturn history," said Aloysius.

"No truth, just the nuclear dust," said Atomic 16.

"Noah Le Gros was a warrior, but that was not an honor because he owned native slaves, and no slaver deserves to be celebrated in history as a wise man," declared Master Jean.

"No wonder the source and translation of his words were obscure," whispered Atomic 16. "Yes, the curse of slavery lasts forever, and the curse of nuclear poison carries on in stories of blood and bone."

11

CASTLE BRAVO

The Space Needle was stupendous, more than five hundred feet high, and hundreds of people waited in line for a fast ride to the observation deck and the spectacular views of Seattle, Mount Baker, Mount Rainier, Lake Washington, Elliott Bay, Glacier Peak, and the Cascade Range.

Nathan bought tickets for everyone, the troupe of veterans and stowaways, to enter the fair and ride to the top of the Space Needle, but the wait time was more than two hours, so the troupe decided to mosey around the exhibitions. Nathan learned from the ticket agent that about twenty thousand people a day waited in line for the Space Needle.

"Tourists standing by for the clouds" said By Now.

"The mongrels are elevator outlaws," wrote Dummy.

"Swarms of sentimental spectators," said Poesy May.

"Tourists wait to favor hearsay," said Prometheus.

Dummy and the stowaways had never seen so many people clustered in one place, and with the loyal mongrels, they were not at ease in the pant and push of the crowds. Pioneer Square and Tilikum Place were chanty ghost scenes compared to the hordes of citizens and tourists from around the world that morning at the World's Fair.

The puppeteers were almost overcome with the crowds at the entrance to the fair and distracted even more with the stream of spectators at the exhibitions. The horde moved slowly from the International Fountain through the worlds of science and commerce and entertainment and grew into a strange anonymous creature with thousands of heads, arms, and tentacles in search of forage, exhibition fantasies, and salvation. The creature surged near the Food Circus and Show Street. The stowaways circled the creature and waited for a suitable space to present hand puppet parleys.

"Too many people at the fair gates," said La Chance.

"More than the entire reservation," said Bad Boy.

"Tourist teases of celebrity," wrote Dummy.

"Turnout for fancy starts and stays," said Big Rant.

"The crowds vanish in the night," said Poesy May.

Aloysius led the way the next morning through the curious pavilions and worlds of science, commerce, art, games, food, and entertainment. The Space Needle was a high and mighty cosmic shadow over the entire landscape of creatures, curiosities, and theme exhibitions of forest products, banking, automobiles, electrical power, oil industry, nations of the world, and a limited choice of religions.

The World of Science surely teased the godly presence of three pavilions, Christian Witness, Sermons from Science, and Christian Science. The churchy hearsay and catchphrases of monotheistic creation were tedious covenants that somehow would defeat the communist demons and curse of the Soviet Union. The various denominations never mentioned the rush of missionaries and colonial slavery, or the pious perpetrators that carried out native separatism on treaty reservations. Not a word, not even slight tributes to the native combat soldiers who served the nation in every war and then waited centuries to be endorsed as citizens of a constitutional democracy.

"Cold war fear and dopey dominance," said By Now.

"Tiresome satires of progress," wrote Dummy.

"Progress is not a place to live," said Toothy.

"Salvation in the radioactive ruins," said Aloysius.

"Denominations of nuclear poison," said Atomic 16.

"Backyard fallout shelters of shame," said Basile.

The Seattle World's Fair was one more continental colony with a merchant deity, a perilous wave of nuclear peace, and space flights of fancy, energy, fashion, and risqué marionettes, nudity, and other bawdy entertainment on Show Street. The only memorable deviation from the crave for science, holy potencies, modern enterprises, and salvation was at the Fine Art Pavilion.

The Northwest Coast native traditional arts, painted totem poles, carved masks, and screens by Tlingit, Haida, Kwakiutl, Tsimshian, and Chinook were presented in the Fine Art Pavilion along with paintings by Willem de Kooning, Paul Klee, Georgia O'Keeffe, Francis Bacon, Jackson Pollock, Claude Monet, John Marin, and Pablo Picasso.

Dummy, Aloysius, and Poesy May wandered through the galleries of great painters. Aloysius was enchanted once again with the magical presence of *Blue Horses* by Franz Marc and the *Sea Piece* by John Marin. Dummy swooned in silence and danced lightly near the *Nymphéas, Water Lilies* by Claude Monet, and then she slowly swayed in the shadows of *Under the Pandanus* by Paul Gauguin. Poesy May was eager, beguiled, and out of breath as she moved closer to the *Woman Seated in Chair* by Pablo Picasso. She was captivated by the contrary grace of visionary contortions and at last turned in silence and gestured in tears of gratitude to others in the gallery.

Aloysius told the troupe over dinner at the *Theatre of Chance* that night about the emotive perceptions of Dummy and the great delights of Poesy May. He related that Picasso created the cubist image, *Woman Seated in Chair*, during the fascist terror of the Nazi Occupation in Paris.

Dummy printed "Lebensraum: Friday, November 5, 1937" on the chalk board, a chapter in *Satie on the Seine: Letters to the Heirs of the Fur Trade*. Basile and Aloysius clearly understood the gesture was to the exposition they had attended in Paris, and they told stories that night about the International Exposition of Art and Technology in Modern Life, *Exposition Internationale des Arts et Techniques dans la Vie Moderne* in 1937.

"The exposition had commissioned eighteen composers to create and record music for more than forty nights along the River Seine in Paris," related Basile. "The conclusion was a wistful and melancholy broadcast of *Fête des Belles Eaux*, or the Festival of Beautiful Waters, composed by Olivier Messiaen.

"The *Fête de la Lumière*, a display of lighted fountains was magical with the sound of the recorded music, and the motion, shimmer, and melancholy shadows that decorated the Palais de Chaillot, the new museums, Musée de l'Homme, Musée de la Marine, and Jardin du Trocadéro, and the majestic five arches of the Pont d'Iena."

"The River Seine inspires poetry," said Poesy May.

"Poets are haunted by rivers," said Prometheus.

"Apollinaire and Le Pont Mirabeau," said Basile.

"The Mississippi River no longer inspires anyone because the river died near the university," said Aloysius. "No magical waves, poetry, or melancholy water music there, and nobody can remember the last lively ripple of clarity or critical gasp of the great river, no one, not me, not you, and the dead river continues to flow but not with great music or poetry."

"The Spanish Civil War continued in abstract art at the *Exposition Internationale*," said Basile. "Adolf Hitler celebrated fascism and the savage removal of Jews."

"Joseph Stalin posed at a great distance with the communists and anarchists on the side of the Spanish Republic," said Nathan. "The savage delusions of Hitler and Stalin, two poseurs of peace and progress, were revealed in the architecture of the pavilion empires at the end of Pont d'Iena."

"The Nazi Pavilion, enclosed in massive pillars of granite, and with no sense of natural motion, faced down the River Seine. An enormous predatory eagle, wings cocked, was perched on the crown of a swastika," said Basile.

"The swastika would be nuclear today," said Bad Boy.

"Fascists of slavery linger in the wings," said Master Jean.

"Reservation agents are everywhere," wrote Dummy.

Dummy, the stowaways, veterans, and mongrels gathered after dinner near the Iron Pergola at Pioneer Square. The night was clear with a brisk breeze from Elliott Bay, and the stories were generous and easy after a long day at the crowded fair. Toothy regretted that he had never visited the great city of Paris at the end of the First World War.

"The Nazi Pavilion floor was coated with red rubber, and Basile and Aloysius refused to set foot in the fascist empire of racial vengeance and book burners," said Nathan.

"The Soviet Pavilion was futuristic, constructed with marble and yet with a sense of light, motion, and, of course, the irony of peace," continued Nathan. "A gigantic sculpture was mounted on the marble prow of the pavilion, and the modern design was by the architect Boris Iofan, a Soviet Jew from Odessa."

"The enormous sculpture, *Worker and Kolkhoz Woman*, by Vera Mukhina, depicted a factory worker, muscular and clearly heroic, with a hammer raised overhead, slanted to the wind, and a sturdy peasant woman with erect nipples, thick streams of hair, and one arm raised with a sickle," said Nathan. "The socialist realism was obvious, but there was no trace of terror in the sculpture or notice of the thousands of factory slaves and peasants that vanished in labor camps." The ironic sculpture, almost eighty feet high, faced the steady flow of the River Seine and the stone pavilion of the fascist Third Reich. Tallulah and the other mongrels bayed over the stories. Dingleberry danced on her back feet around the Iron Pergola.

"The new fascists are scientists who design deadly nuclear weapons, and the world is much more dangerous today than the desperate years between the two world wars," said Atomic 16.

The thousands of visitors at the *Exposition Internationale* sauntered over the Pont d'Iena and paused between the two pavilions of social realism, communism, and the brute force of fascist vengeance, and never cursed out loud about the fascist architecture of the Soviet Union and the German Reich as the absolute demonic reveals of national terror and another world war.

"Sometimes world expositions convey the obvious rise of fascism in design and architecture of gaunt political structures and statuary, and today, close at hand, the big tents and folding chairs of evangelical caravans bear witness to the rise of a new fascism," said Nathan. "Seattle is an exposition of contenders, more science, space, and futurity than the extreme nook and cranny fascists or the authoritarian hearsay of evangelists."

The Christian Witness Pavilion was located near the United States Science Pavilion, and the promotion of science and godly creation continued with the tedious tournament of theories about causation, divine faith, human evolution, biblical trust, relativity, demonic tumbles, earthly wobbles, and cosmic chance.

The Christian Witness leaflet proclaimed that the "whole program will be keyed to the theme, 'Jesus Christ—The Same, Yesterday, Today, and Forever,' seeking to make Christian faith meaningful to the scientific and futuristic emphasis of the Exposition."

"Hallelujah to the churchy scribes," shouted Basile.

"Hallelujah cash from the witnesses," said Bad Boy.

"Hallelujah three times because the angels of glory eloped with space masters and nuclear scientists at the science pavilion," said La Chance.

The United States Science Exhibit presented "the exciting story of science in a show unlike any ever seen before. It combines the techniques of a dozen graphic and theater arts, is part historical drama, part laboratory, part magic, and all science. It crosses time and space as it takes audiences into the ocean depths and to the outer galaxies, from the beginning of the scientific era in the next century. It has as its dual aims 'to present the role of man in a search for truth in science' and to 'stimulate youths' interest in science."

"Science is a magical road show," said Master Jean.

"More creative than churchy liturgy," said Bad Boy.

Billy Graham, the evangelist and high wire crusader of godly favors, preached to more than twenty thousand people at the World's Fair last Sunday, and the churchy highs of hallelujah lingered in every pavilion for several days, and even on Show Street. Graham visited the religious and science pavilions and later denounced a puppet show because the "women don't wear bras." The women without bras were short wooden marionettes in *Les Poupées de Paris*, a popular performance of bawdy puppets on Show Street.

"Billy Graham would no doubt object to nude mannequins in the backrooms of department stores," mocked By Now.

Native Northwest Coast art was evocative, and the eternal images and scenes of great cultures continued in the creative visions of artists. The other direct reference to natives was the mock Indian Village on Show Street. The narrow space near the arena and stadium was reserved mainly for risqué shows, the Gay Nineties Review, Paris Spectacular, Peeps Backstage, and Girls of the Galaxy, which was favored, censured, and closed twice because nudity was ruled intolerable by the managers of the fair.

Master Jean fashioned two cloth hand puppets, Edward Teller, the heart of stone theoretical physicist at the Lawrence Livermore National Laboratory in California, and the other hand puppet represented the twenty-three sailors who were on board an ocean fishing boat named the *Daigo Fukuryū Maru*, Fifth Lucky Dragon. The two cloth hand puppets, one huge and the other slender and peaky, carried out a critical parley near the five arched towers of the United States Science Pavilion. The arches simulated modernist cathedrals and demonstrated in architecture the spectacular contests of science and the churchy hearsay of the Second Coming at the World's Fair.

"Nuclear outrage over hearsay destiny," said Atomic 16.

"Postcard Mary creates hearsay liberty," wrote Dummy.

The Japanese sailors on the Lucky Dragon were absolutely exposed to the radioactive blast, ash, and white rain from the detonation of Castle Bravo, a thermonuclear weapon tested at Bikini Atoll. The detonation was a thousand times more intense than Little Boy, the atomic bomb that destroyed Hiroshima, and Fat Man, the atomic bomb that destroyed Nagasaki.

Dummy posted the chalk board with a new dream song on the front bumper of the *Theatre of Chance*. Early the next morning Big Rant and Poesy May chanted the song in harmony and with repetitions of the phrases.

nuclear war stories
hiroshima the death of totems
castle bravo alights in the blood
dream songs in the clouds
waiting for wovoka

Master Jean practiced the dramatic gestures of the hand puppets, and Atomic 16 was eager to shout out the actual words, phrases, and guttural quotations of the thermonuclear terrorist Edward Teller. Poesy May lowered her voice and chanted the haunting phrase *shi no hai*, ashes of death, twenty-three times as a solemn aria in a nuclear opera of hand puppets that honored the crew of the Lucky Dragon. Dummy raised her hands and gently conducted the six mongrels to moan and bay in perfect harmony as a great choir in a tragic opera of Japanese fisherman exposed to the radioactive contamination of a thermonuclear weapon.

TELLER: People were warned of radioactivity.
LUCKY CREW: *Shi no hai.*
TELLER: The explosion was underestimated.
LUCKY CREW: Ashes of death.
TELLER: The direction of the wind changed.
LUCKY CREW: *Shi no hai.*
TELLER: Islands in the Pacific got some of the radiation.
LUCKY CREW: Ashes of death.
TELLER: Many natives were exposed to radioactivity.
LUCKY CREW: *Shi no hai.*
TELLER: None got sick.

LUCKY CREW: Ashes of death.

TELLER: Japanese fishing boat got rained upon.

LUCKY CREW: *Shi no hai.*

TELLER: Couple of hundred miles away.

LUCKY CREW: Ashes of death.

TELLER: *Daigo Fukuryū Maru.*

LUCKY CREW: *Shi no hai.*

TELLER: The Fifth Lucky Dragon.

LUCKY CREW: Ashes of death.

TELLER: We had instructed boats not to go there.

LUCKY CREW: *Shi no hai.*

TELLER: Those people got quite sick.

LUCKY CREW: Ashes of death.

TELLER: One of them died of the effects of radiation.

LUCKY CREW: *Shi no hai.*

TELLER: Now to my mind it is remarkable.

LUCKY CREW: Ashes of death.

TELLER: Remarkable that this one death shocked Americans.

LUCKY CREW: *Shi no hai.*

TELLER: Shocked Americans more than Hiroshima.

LUCKY CREW: Ashes of death.

TELLER: Enormous and unjustifiable fears of radioactivity.

LUCKY CREW: *Shi no hai.*

TELLER: That fear was already there.

LUCKY CREW: Ashes of death.

TELLER: We know that a lot of radioactivity is harmful.

LUCKY CREW: *Shi no hai.*

TELLER: Low levels of radioactivity appear to be helpful.

LUCKY CREW: Ashes of death.

TELLER: Rather than harmful.

LUCKY CREW: *Shi no hai.*

TELLER: Radioactivity has been greatly exaggerated.

LUCKY CREW: Ashes of death.

TELLER: Greatly and improperly exaggerated.

LUCKY CREW: *Shi no hai.*

Three security officers moved strategically through the audience under the five arches. The fair guards were prepared to respectfully remove the puppet master and the mongrel choir at the very moment that Atomic 16 shouted the words of Edward Teller, "Shocked Americans more than Hiroshima." The officers paused, turned slowly, considered the empathy of the audience, and decided to wait and take notice of the entire puppet parley. At the end, the officers, along with the enthusiastic spectators, praised the hand puppet mockery and denounced the words of Edward Teller.

The melancholy sound of a distant bugle was heard at the end of the puppet parley, a salute to the sailors of the Lucky Dragon. Master Jean was standing at the far end of the science pavilion near the pond and fountain, and he slowly played the Last Post. Hearsay was hushed, and the wistful notes brought tears to the eyes of every veteran near the grand arches.

"Last Post of nuclear terror," said Nathan.

"Last Post of nuclear fission," said Basile.

"Last Post of radioactive milk," said By Now.

"Last Post of atomic test fallout," said Atomic 16.

"Last Post of lonesome veterans," said Aloysius.

"Last Post of nuclear arms," said La Chance.

"Last Post of combat poetry," wrote Dummy.

"Last Post of ashes and death," said Poesy May.

Poesy May remembered the short poem "The Last Post" by Robert Graves, the Irish poet who served with the Royal Welch Fusiliers in the First World War. Poesy recited a few phrases of the poem, "The bugler sent a call of high romance," and the dead "in a row with the other broken ones," and the last line, "Jolly young Fusiliers too good to die," and then she read out loud a dream song that afternoon by Dummy.

> *bugler last post*
> *ghosts in a dream song*
> *ashes of death*
> *nightly scenes of nuclear terror*
> *natives too good to die*

Pioneer Square was haunted with the sound of distant buglers and the remembrance of war that night, even the best heart stories of the fair were blunted by the parley, *shi no hai*, the ashes of death. The mongrels were perceptive and always ready to hush a bark and bay away the ghosts of bloody scenes in the nightmares of any war. The mongrels moaned and then moved closer that night to Atomic 16.

12

Tumble Names

The Elliott Bay haze moved slowly ashore with no mercy and covered the bodies of broken men with a slight shroud of menace and secrecy. The distant moan of ferry boats merged with the watery gasps and raspy coughs along the backstreets and in abandoned buildings near Pioneer Square. Nothing mattered more to the forsaken men that cold morning than military blankets or give away crazy quilts, and in the doorways of empty stores, a few stray veterans were covered with nothing more than limp copies of daily newspapers.

Dummy sat on a camp chair in the ruins of the Iron Pergola and carved from a block of fallen birch the great wrinkled face of the author Samuel Beckett. Hail Mary and George Eliot were the only mongrels at her side as chips of wood covered the creased theatre placard with a photograph of the novelist and playwright. Dummy carved with care the great curved furrows on his brow and created a dream song at the same time.

> stowaway beckett
> outwitted occupation fascists
> weathered betrayals
> theatre favors
> waiting for the unnamable

Basile and Aloysius had attended the first production of the play *En Attendant Godot* by Samuel Beckett at the Théâtre de Babylone in Paris. Nathan reminded them that *Waiting for Godot* was reviewed at the time with favor by Sylvain Zegel in *La Libération*. Beckett was an author "who can animate his characters so vividly that the audience identifies with them, suffering and laughing with them."

Since that first production, the esoteric play has been staged in great cities around the world and at San Quentin State Prison in California, but not always with the same favor, promise, and audience enthusiasm as the first production eight years after the end of the Second World War in Paris.

"The audience at the Théâtre de Babylone was haunted by the horror of violence and vengeance, and the everlasting shame of those who collaborated with the enemy and betrayed friends and family," said Nathan. He declared that no author could easily conceive or represent in dramatic characters the actual terror and anomie of the moment, or even cope with the feigned colors of patriots and the deceptive diction of fascist terrorism, or simply show the constant brunt of betrayal during the Nazi Occupation of France.

Samuel Beckett was a furtive translator and served as a courier in *La Résistance,* and later he created the elusive sense of cultural absence with two characters, Estragon and Vladimir, who were exiled in a satire of shame and suicide in the desolation of civilization and liberty. The audience was inexplicably relieved from the memory of familiar collaborators and the capitulation of ethos during the fascist occupation and the Vichy Regime. The literary favors of discontent and understated rage were recited in the terse hearsay dialogue of an original play about the memory of nothing, and the petulant wait, wait, wait for Godot.

"Treaty discontent over morsels," wrote Dummy.

"Fascist travel brochures," said Master Jean.

"Collaboration as salvation," shouted Big Rant.

"Vichy celebrities of nothing," said Prometheus.

"Beckett probably never met a native, but the parleys he created in *Waiting for Godot* are similar to the wait over treaties and natives over panic holes," said Aloysius.

"The irony of silence in panic holes," said By Now.

"Panic hearsay at the post office," said Aloysius.

"Waiting for marvelous hearsay," said Master Jean.

"Postcard Mary was our Godot," wrote Dummy.

"Beckett waits for Jean Racine," said Nathan.

"Beckett waits for Nancy Cunard," said Basile.

"Why wait for the Cunard?" asked Big Rant.

"She published his first poem," said Aloysius.

"Throwing Jesus out of the skylight," said Nathan.

"Samuel Beckett must be more French than Irish, and more Ojibwe than French, and at last he was a moody native heir of the ancient fur trade," said Basile.

"Beckett is a literary coureur de bois," shouted Nathan.

Nathan contacted the manager of the Seattle World's Fair Playhouse and obtained seats in the third row for the Actor's Workshop of San Francisco production of *Waiting for Godot*. The seats were close enough to grasp the nuance of diction and to clearly see the facial gestures of the actors. The audience was much too quiet and polite during the performance and then, after a gracious applause, silently marched out of the Playhouse. Dummy created several dream songs that night after the play but printed only one and leaned the chalk board on the windshield of the bus.

nothing to be done
fright is scarcely reasonable
suicide in every scene
words lost to shame
theatre slights and silence

The stowaways had read sections of *Waiting for Godot* out loud and selected phrases for a puppet parley with the author Samuel Beckett. Poesy May, Bad Boy, and La Chance sat next to each other in the Playhouse and secretly mocked the pithy talk back of Estragon and Vladimir. The stowaways were prepared for an ironic puppet parley a few days later with Sitting Bull and Samuel Beckett at Tilikum Place near the stone face of a bear and the statue of Chief Seattle.

Sitting Bull, the Hunkpapa Lakota visionary and resistance warrior, envisioned the casualties of the Seventh Cavalry at the Battle of the Little Big Horn and celebrated with thousands of native warriors the death of General George Armstrong Custer. Sitting Bull honored the solemn scare and sway of the Sun Dance, and later he praised the peace and solace of the Ghost Dance Religion.

"Waiting for Wovoka," wrote Dummy.

"Waiting for Samuel Beckett," said Nathan.

"Waiting for Nancy Cunard," said Aloysius.

"Waiting for nothing," said Prometheus.

Native puppets were the great celebrities of nothing, and the hand talk parleys were catchy scenes of mockery that overturned manners with only the slightest gestures and the easy sway, jerk, and bounce of wood, cloth, contrived debris, and the paper heads of hand puppets.

"Summer heart stories, dream songs, and tumble names of hand puppets, rescued natives from the curse of cultural models that were roughed
out with blood quanta by government agents and anthropologists," said Basile. "The puppet mockery of the churchy promises of salvation were en-
actments of nothing, and the exaltations of nothing haunted the priests and
federal agents, but they could never decide how to sideline the clever stories of native totems and mongrel loyalty or the unreserved sense of liberty
with hand puppets in a literary parley."

Dummy raised two new puppets, Sitting Bull on her left hand and Samuel Beckett on her right hand. Big Rant slowly removed the black velvet
shrouds and revealed the pensive features of a native visionary and the
handsome furrows on the brow of a poet, novelist, and playwright. Beckett wore a black cravat and spectacles with wire frames. Sitting Bull wore
a coarse white shirt and a feather in his braided hair, the simulated golden
eagle feather of a warrior. Sitting Bull slowly turned to the side and bowed
to a woman in the audience who was worried about her curious child and
the mysterious enchantment of puppets. Samuel Beckett gestured to Master Jean who raised his bugle and played the First Call.

Prometheus wagged his fingers in white gloves and roused the audience
that gathered around the statue of Chief Seattle. Bad Boy and Big Rant
selected the lines from the strange colloquy of Estragon and Vladimir in
Waiting for Godot. La Chance was the benign voice of Samuel Beckett
for the characters Estragon and Vladimir, and Poesy May was the solemn
voice of the visionary Sitting Bull. Dummy summoned the five mongrels to
sit at her side, turned the superbly carved hand puppets face to face, and
the parley started with the actual translation of comments by Sitting Bull.

SITTING BULL: You come here to tell us lies.

ESTRAGON: Nothing to be done.

SITTING BULL: We don't want to hear them.

ESTRAGON: Nothing to be done.

SITTING BULL: The whites may get me at last.

VLADIMIR: To be dead is not enough for them.

SITTING BULL: What treaty that the whites have kept has the red
man broken? Not one. What treaty that the white man ever made
with us have they kept? Not one.

VLADIMIR: Let us make the most of it, before it is too late!

TALLULAH: Wild harmonic contralto bay.

SITTING BULL: What white man can say I never stole his land or a penny of his money? Yet they say that I am a thief.

VLADIMIR: You should have been a poet.

SITTING BULL: The life of the white man is slavery. They are prisoners in towns and farms. The life my people want is a life of freedom.

ESTRAGON: We weren't made for the same road.

SITTING BULL: You are fools to make yourselves slaves to a piece of fat bacon, some hardtack, and a little sugar and coffee.

ESTRAGON: We have no rights anymore.

SITTING BULL: I am nothing, neither a chief nor a soldier.

ESTRAGON: No, nothing is certain.

SITTING BULL: We want no white men here. The Black Hills belong to me. If the whites try to take them, I will fight.

ESTRAGON: All the dead voices.

SITTING BULL: I will remain what I am until I die, a hunter, and when there are no buffalo or other game, I will send my children to hunt and live on the prairie.

VLADIMIR: Yes, in this immense confusion one thing is clear, we are waiting for Godot to come.

SITTING BULL: I hate all the white people. You are thieves and liars. You have taken away our land and made us outcasts.

VLADIMIR: To every man his little cross.

GEORGE ELIOT: Singular soprano bays.

SITTING BULL: If the Great Spirit had desired me to be a white man, he would have made me so in the first place.

ESTRAGON: Do you think God sees me?

DINGLEBERRY: Danced in a circle and yodeled.

SITTING BULL: Let us put our minds together and see what life we can make for our children.

VLADIMIR: Beginning to come around to that opinion.

SITTING BULL: It does not take many words to tell the truth.

VLADIMIR: This is becoming really insignificant.

SITTING BULL: These people have made many rules that the rich may break but the poor may not. They take their tithes from the poor and weak to support the rich and those who rule.

ESTRAGON: People are bloody ignorant apes.

TALLULAH: Wild harmonic contralto bay.

SITTING BULL: Each man is good in the sight of the Great Spirit. It is not necessary that eagles should be crows.

VLADIMIR: Blaming on the boots the faults of the feet.

SITTING BULL: Inside me are two dogs. One is mean and evil and the other is good and they must fight each other all the time. When asked which one wins I answer, the one I feed the most.

VLADIMIR: Then all the dogs came running.

DANIEL: Raised his head, sneezed, barked, and moaned.

SITTING BULL: I have killed, robbed, and injured too many white men to believe in a good peace.

ESTRAGON: What about hanging ourselves?

SITTING BULL: I wish it to be remembered that I was the last man of my tribe to surrender my rifle.

VLADIMIR: It'd give me an erection.

SITTING BULL: A warrior I have been. Now it is all over.

ESTRAGON: Nothing to be done.

Two older men and a young woman in the audience talked back and mocked the gestures of the two puppets, and at the end, other people reached out to touch the carved birch faces of Sitting Bull and Samuel Beckett. Dummy was the center of attention for a short time, but when she covered the puppets with velvet and only bowed in response to praise or questions about the parley several people stared back in silence and then walked away.

Master Jean circled the statue of Chief Seattle and once more played the First Call as Prometheus waved the audience back to the statue to hear a theatrical recitation of the very last long sentence from *The Unnamable* by Samuel Beckett. Big Rant chanted the narrative of strange alibis, teases of mood and manner, sentiments of an equivocal existence, lost words, trace of promises, tumble names and uncertainty, evasive gestures and word play, the surprise of thresholds, and the clever curves of literary motion in the novel.

"They're going to abandon me, it will be the silence, for a moment, a good few moments, or it will be mine, the lasting one, that didn't last, that still lasts, it will be I, you must go on, I can't go on, you must go on, I'll go on, you must say words, as long as there are any, until they find me, until they say to me, strange pain, strange sin, you must go on, perhaps it's done already, perhaps they have said me already, perhaps they have carried me to the threshold of my story, before the door that opens on my story, that would surprise me, if it opens, it will be I, it will be the silence, where I am, I don't know, I'll never know, in the silence you don't know, you must go on, I can't go on, I'll go on."

"Going on is natural motion," wrote Dummy.

"The stowaways must go on," shouted Master Jean.

"Trickery of creation stories must go on," said Big Rant.

Dummy was honored for the marvelous gestures of Sitting Bull and Samuel Beckett that night over dinner of fresh salmon and roasted potatoes at the *Theatre of Chance*. The puppet parley of selected comments, confessions, and pretense of revelations were mocked with delight by the stowaways.

"Someone said me already," said La Chance.

"Many people have said me," wrote Dummy.

"Who knows how we must go on," said Poesy May.

"My story always surprises me," shouted Big Rant.

"Fur traders can't go on, shouldn't have gone on, but they go on, they go on to slaughter totemic animals," said Bad Boy.

Dummy laughed in silence, raised her hands to praise the wise mockery, and wrote on the chalk board, "You must go on, I can't go on, I'll go on with the mongrels and stowaways." At the same time, she denounced the easy chitchat surrender to suicide by Estragon and Vladimir. Hail Mary turned to bay, George Eliot moaned, Daniel barked, and Dingleberry yodeled and danced in circles. Dummy wrote an ironic dream song that night.

> *samuel beckett*
> *walks in the clouds*
> *estragon might hang himself*
> *vladimir waits for an erection*
> *godot is a snow ghost*

The *Theatre of Chance* had been parked for more than two weeks near Pioneer Square. Day after day a few more veterans visited the bus and told hesitant and evasive stories of combat and the cold nights on Elliott Bay. Master Jean teased the easy course of cold nights stories, and worried that some veterans might change war stories with the seasons. "How many cold night stories are for the trust and charity, and with that fairly done, why not overturn a war scene and mock the war away?"

"Radiation turned me cold forever," said Atomic 16.

"Mockery never landed in my memories," said Toothy.

"Charity is the satire of the gods," said Prometheus.

"Mock the wars and the stories stay," said Aloysius.

"Heart stories are more than memories, more than hearsay or daily headlines, and never measured by temperatures or the season," wrote Dummy. "Native heart stories and mockery are inevitable, tease and irony are necessary, and sometimes warm memories are nothing more than dopey nostalgia."

Some veterans listened and never told stories, some waited only to hear the stories of others about the wars that never seem to end, the wars of memory, and the generous tease of native stories at the Iron Pergola and *Theatre of Chance*. The mockery of missions, warfare, and enemies were crucial, and some desolate veterans never envisioned the scenes of combat, fear, and death as the practice of memory or ironic stories.

Dummy printed concise notes on the chalk board several times a day and expected the stowaways to read every word and to remember the sentiments of the messages, such as this note, "Hearsay postcards are more memorable than catechism," and, "Reservations are the dumping grounds for remorse, feigned guilt, and nostalgia." Basile copied most of the aphorisms and reveals of her native heart stories.

The pithy philosophical declarations were selected for a quirky puppet parley with three hand puppets, Dummy, Samuel Beckett, and By Now. Dummy had carved the puppets for other puppet parleys, and now as a surprise the same puppets were ready to tease and talk back to the chalk board declarations. The obscure responses to the incisive chalk board notes were selected with concern by Poesy May and Big Rant from *The Unnamable* by Samuel Beckett.

The puppet parley tease was staged on a balmy night near the Iron Pergola at Pioneer Square. Big Rant raised Dummy on her right hand, the only puppet with round cheeks and gray hair, and shouted out selected chalk board aphorisms. Poesy May raised the puppet with blue eyes and the furrowed brow and she was the quiet voice of Samuel Beckett. By Now was the actual voice of the hand puppet By Now.

DUMMY: Puppets are the great celebrities of nothing.

BECKETT: They're going to abandon me.

BY NOW: Federal agents are the celebrities of mockery.

BECKETT: I never stop speaking, but sometimes too low, too far away, too far within, to hear, no, I hear, to understand, not that I ever understand. It fades, it goes in, behind the door, I'm going silent, there's going to be silence, I'll listen, it's worse than speaking no, no worse, no better.

DUMMY: Natives shout dreams into the clouds only to stay.

BECKETT: I should have liked to go silent first, there were moments I thought that would be my reward for having spoken so long and so saliently, to enter living into silence.

BY NOW: Beckett understands the silence of hand puppets.

BECKETT: I want to go silent, it wants to go silent, it can't, it does for a second, then it starts again, that's not the real silence, it says that's not the real silence, what can be said of the real silence, I don't know, that I don't know what it is, that there is no such thing, that perhaps there is such a thing, yes, that perhaps there is, somewhere, I'll never know.

DUMMY: Silent mockery is the voice of native liberty.

BECKETT: You must say words, as long as there are any.

BY NOW: Long enough to ridicule federal agents and fascists.

BECKETT: How can I say it, that's all words, they're all I have, and not many of them, the words fail, the voice fails, so be it, I know that well, it will be the silence, full of murmurs, distant cries, the usual silence, spent listening, spent waiting, waiting for the voice.

DUMMY: Never shame a hesitant child with silence.

BECKETT: Nothing ever troubles me. And yet I am troubled. Nothing has ever changed since I have been here. But I dare not infer from this that nothing ever will change.

BY NOW: Tease mongrels and shy students with care.

BECKETT: One starts things moving without a thought of how to stop them. In order to speak. One starts speaking as if it were possible to stop at will. It is better so. The search for the means to put an end to things, an end to speech, is what enables the discourse to continue. No, I must not try to think, simply utter. Method or no method I shall have to banish them in the end, the beings, things, shapes, sounds, and lights with which my haste to speak has encumbered this place. In the frenzy of utterance the concern with truth.

DUMMY: Reservations are the dumping grounds for remorse and nostalgia.

BECKETT: I never knew, to have them carry me into my story, the words that remain, my old story, which I've forgotten, far from here, through the noise, through the door, into the silence, that must be it, it's too late, perhaps it's too late, perhaps they have, how would I know, in the silence you don't know, in the silence you don't know, it's the door, perhaps I'm at the door, that would surprise me.

DUMMY: Puppet parleys are hearsay dream songs.

BECKETT: I can't go on, you must go on, I'll go on, you must say words, as long as there are any, until they find me, until they say me, strange pain, strange sin, you must go on, perhaps it's done already, perhaps they have said me already, perhaps they have carried me to the threshold of my story, before the door that opens on my story, that would surprise me, if it opens, it will be I, it will be the silence.

DUMMY: My silence is the threshold of every native story.

BECKETT: Where I am, I don't know.

DUMMY: No fancy feigns of cultural confidence, no plots, praise, or promises of salvation, only the words, the silence of my words, the visionary words of natural motion in dream songs.

BECKETT: Ah if only this voice could stop, this meaningless voice
    which prevents you from being nothing and nowhere.
DUMMY: Silent words are natural motion and liberty.
BECKETT: In silence you don't know, you must go on. I can't go on,
    you must go on, I'll go on.

The Pioneer Square audience was more at ease and receptive with the
puppet parley than the weary spectators at Tilikum Place near the World's
Fair, and the mongrels were accustomed to the easy pace of casual tourists
near the Tlingit Totem Pole and the Iron Pergola. The people on the street
that night were scarcely worried about time or bound to episodes of cultural
promises as they waited with anticipation for the original presentation of
hand puppets.

The veterans, backstreet roamers, workers, and curious tourists at Pioneer Square saluted the three carved hand puppets and applauded the
marvelous chorus of mongrel bays, muted barks, harmonious moans, and
body bumps, and most of the people at the parley countered with hesitant silence the strange phrases and sudden gestures of the hand puppet
Samuel Beckett. The puppet colloquies were unstable literary diversions,
vaguely cast down, deftly ironic, and at the same time, the teases of words
and moody back talk were praised by other spectators, especially those who
shared the charm of elusive diction, sentence crops, and literary maneuvers
in the novels *Ulysses* and *Finnegans Wake* by James Joyce.

"Beckett ain't the way we talk around here, he's a tricky book talker, not
a street talker and he ain't the talkers we know," said a stout delivery man in
a gray uniform.

"I was worried at first and then tormented by the hesitations and moody
scenes about silence, but the incredible back talk was enchanting, and
phrase by phrase my moods turned to solitude and melancholy," shouted a
woman in a bright red raincoat.

"Yes, and the uneasy counter play of silence turned into a strange retreat,
a kind of get away poetry, and yet the cause to grieve was nothing more than
the secrecy of silence," said a poet and bookstore clerk. "Maybe the wordy
struggles over silence and shame became an incredible sense of regret and
sorrow, and more than enough misery to make me cry."

"Never heard anyone talk like that, but loved the gestures of the puppets, especially the great round face and wispy white hair of the puppet named Dummy," said an elementary school teacher on vacation from South Dakota.

"Beckett is more of a puppet trickster talker than a teacher, butcher, or rancher, and that's just fine with me for a change, at least he doesn't talk like nervous radio announcers or the vacant chitchat of tourists at the exhibitions of the World's Fair," said a restaurant waiter and a sailor on Elliott Bay.

"Dummy is my favorite, the wild hair and silence, the grand silence, and she made me feel at home with pithy notes and quick gestures of a generous puppet, the silent soul of a puppet in the presence of a cut and run contender of wayward words," said a tall young man with blonde hair who was a lecturer of rhetoric at a community college.

Dummy was at ease and certain with silence and has never betrayed the peace of her native lover Nookaa who was burned to ashes in the Great Hinckley Fire. She has shouted out, mourned, laughed, celebrated, and teased the mongrels only in silence, and has never voiced the actual sound of a single word for more than sixty years. She was secure in the spirit of silence and carried on with a sense of courage.

"Plucky silence is easy, of course, and then a mystical silence and solitude becomes an everlasting tribute and constant memory of my tender lover Nookaa," wrote Dummy.

Dummy turned her head from side to side, smiled at the audience, covered the hand puppets with black velvet, and then returned to the *Theatre of Chance*. Much later the loyal mongrels gathered at her side when she placed the Silvertone hand crank record player on a bench near the Iron Pergola. She leaned back in a rickety camp chair and listened at full volume to the sublime spinto soprano voice of Renata Tebaldi in the magnificent opera *La Bohème* by Giacomo Puccini.

Renata Tebaldi sang the arias "Sì mi chiamano Mimì" in the first act and "Quando me'n vò" in the second act of *La Bohème*. Her clear soprano voice resounded in cold and desolate alleys and vacant buildings, calmed the wild boasts, overcame the easy chatter, subdued simulations, and easily changed the natural course of ordinary conversations on James Street and Yesler Way at Pioneer Square.

Dummy cleaned the record, played the arias a second time, and gestured in silence the magical tones of the soprano voice in the shadows of the Iron Pergola. George Eliot, Trophy Bay, and Hail Mary leaned closer to the camp chair, raised their heads, and delivered a harmonious bay. The other mongrels softly moaned and bayed as a chorus in the spinto traces of the marvelous arias.

MUSETTA'S WALTZ

Quando me'n vó soletta per la via
When walking alone through the streets
La gente sosta e mira
People stop and stare
E la bellezza mia tutta ricerca in me
And look at my beauty
Da capo a piè...
From head to foot
Ed assaporo allor la bramosia
And then I savor the subtle desire
Sottil, che da gli occhi traspira
Which transpires from their eyes
E dai palesi vezzi intender sa
And from the obvious charms they perceive
Alle occulte beltà
The hidden beauty
Così l'effluvio del desìo tutta m'aggira
So the scent of desire is all around me
Felice mi fa!
It makes me happy!
E tu che sai, che memori e ti struggi
And you, knowing, reminding and longing
Da me tanto rifuggi
You shrink from me.
So ben,
I know it well,
Le angoscie tue non la vuoi dir,
You don't want to express your anguish.

Ma ti senti morir!
But you feel like you're dying.

Dummy was fast asleep in the rickety camp chair when Renata Tebaldi sang the line *"Da me tanto rifuggi"* near the end of the aria. The hand crank record player had not been wound for the second round of arias and the clear soprano timbre slowed down to mere moans. Tallulah and Trophy Bay raised their heads and gently moaned with the slow tones of the aria, slower and slower, and the other mongrels united as a chorus of drones to accompany the soprano undertones.

Renata Tebaldi slowly lost her voice that night, the mongrel moans turned to gentle groans, and the bay haze rounded the lights over the Iron Pergola. The grand spirits of native chance shimmered in the early seasons of the night and then leaned into the easy shadows of natural motion. Dummy turned her head and sighed in the camp chair. Dingleberry shivered and sneezed, and one more perfect night of native heart stories ended with an opera at Pioneer Square.

ABOUT THE AUTHOR

Gerald Vizenor is a prolific novelist, poet,
literary critic, and citizen of the White Earth
Nation of the Anishinaabeg in Minnesota. His
novels *Shrouds of White Earth* and *Griever:
An American Monkey King in China* won
American Book Awards, and the latter
also earned a New York Fiction
Collective Award.